Coral Eyeshadow

EMILIE **TSCHANZ**

novum ◢ pro

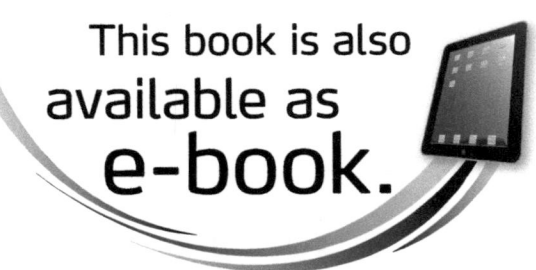

www.novum-publishing.co.uk

© 2022 novum publishing

ISBN 978-3-99131-424-0
Editing: Roderick Pritchard-Smith
Cover photos: Johanna Goodyear, Danazurki, Prostockstudio, Pattadis Walarput | Dreamstime.com
Cover design, layout & typesetting: novum publishing

www.novum-publishing.co.uk

Climate neutral
Print product
ClimatePartner.com/16547-2201-1002

EVERY STORY STARTS SOMEWHERE

There was no sign of the sun, and the skies were filled with bulky grey clouds. A thick layer of smog loomed in the air. The weather was depressing just like my mood. It was a Monday, which meant that I had to make my way to work. I didn't like that, not at all. Maybe, it was because what I was doing was illegal or maybe it was because my boss was a total ass. Anyway, I was only doing it for the money, and it was kind of worth it since I couldn't get a job anywhere else because of my past. I was kind of grateful for this job. Or was I? Well, I let myself think I was. All I could smell was wet cardboard and cigarette smoke when I entered the factory, where I worked. It was hidden in the woods in the middle of nowhere. It was one of those places that no one could find if they weren't looking for it. Well, even if they were searching for it, they probably wouldn't be able to find it. I personally hoped no one was hunting this place down. I actually hoped that no one knew about it. I made my way up to the second floor. The stairs were always a challenge for me because I had lost one of my legs approximately ten years ago.

When I finally managed to get to the top of the cement staircase, I took a deep breath before I hobbled along the long hallway to my boss's office at the end of the hall. Upon entering, the first thing that I heard was the loud and powerful voice of my boss. I started getting a sicking feeling in my stomach, even though this was normal behaviour for him, it still made me feel uncomfortable. He gave me a wry smile, his eyes were glowing but not in a good way. His smug face disgusted me and filled me with anger. I could feel my insides boiling up and wanting to punch his face.

'Your're work is well below what we want! Watch out or we'll whack you!'

That was a normal thing my boss would say to me. The first time I had heard those words, I had been perplexed but not anymore. Now I was just uncomfortable and angry, very angry. I continued to listen to my assignments for the day and then went off to my lab to start working.

I was in charge of creating the recipes to produce counterfeit beauty products and other things that I did not want to make. It did not really matter what was mixed in those cosmetics. All that mattered was that they were quick, easy, and cheap to produce. I knew that I used toxic substances that caused health issues. However, I didn't care. I used to care but my concern about everything when it comes to my emotions have faded, especially my feelings towards these beauty products. They were just objects to me. First of all, I was not the one using these kinds of cosmetics, secondly, I really needed the money, thirdly I was afraid of leaving, and last but not least, I could not get a legitimate job because of my criminal history and my missing ID. So that is why I was stuck doing this job. Despite that I hated doing illegal counterfeiting, but I must admit, I was pretty good at it. The production of the drugs was another story. I hated doing it even more than the cosmetics. The cosmetics were giving people rashes, harming their lungs maybe, intoxicating their skin. But they weren't contributing to a drug epidemic, they weren't killing thousands of people. I just could not get the picture out of my mind of a teenager taking these pills or whatever else I was asked to mix together. Then they would either get hooked, addicted for life or die or end up in a hospital. To me this was horrible, like what the fuck was I doing with my life. I tried not to think about it but that was not all too easy. They weren't the drugs we used to have like pot or heroin. They were chemical party drugs, stronger, more addictive and a lot more dangerous. I just wish I did not have to do it, I wish I could turn back time.

I was once considered to be a decent, upright person or that is at least what I think. I had completed my master's in chemistry and had finished top of my class. Sadly, back then, I had become friends with Mike and my once perfect life was destroyed bit by bit.

I was working on an eyeshadow that could sell for eighty dollars but could be produced for thirty cents. That was insufficient for my boss. He always wanted more. He wanted the impossible. The thing was, he did nothing the whole day and earned millions of dollars while the rest of us worked for three dollars an hour and were treated like slaves. We all stuck around for the torture because we couldn't do anything better with our lives. More importantly we were afraid of the consequences of leaving. I wish I could turn back time and go back to my nice little apartment in New York with my well-paid job but that's simply just not possible. Impossible, and due to my numerous bad decisions, I have ended up here. Every single day, I work for ten hours, with just one fifteen-minute break. And every day, I think about how stupid and blind I must have been as a student as a student to have agreed with Mike. I should have not listened to the things he said. I should have known better. I should have suspected that all he wanted was to cover his own ass and continue with his illegal business. He never had any intentions of becoming a better person. Be that as it may be, I had been vulnerable. He had a life plan to become the one of the richest men in the world, in a not very legitimate way. Well maybe at first, he had intended to do it through a respectable career but, well, what can I say? He didn't. And for all the things he did he would send others to prison and probably still does. Well actually, I know he still does. I know it. He had this manipulative way and was brilliant at persuading people to follow his orders. He had always looked so professional in his suits with his perfectly groomed black hair. Moreover, his eyes, his eyes were out of this world. If you looked into them, you would imagine someone genuine with a warm, giving heart. However, light blue eyes can fool people or at least they fooled me. They still sometimes do.

In the lab, I was mixing mercury, a heavy metal, into my eyeshadow powder when my 'friend' Lilian came in to bring me the cyanide I had asked for. Lilian was in charge of organizing the supplies to make the cosmetics. She looked really rough on the outside, but she was actually really nice on the inside. She had a big scar across her face and tattoos and piercings that covered her body. In addition to that, half of her red hair was shaved off and the remaining hair was cut into a weird zig-zag patterns. Maybe she just wanted to look rebellious, or it was a phase in her life. I remember when I was nineteen, I definitely would not have walked the streets looking like that and believe me, I had my teenage phase. Lilian ended up here because when she was sixteen, she washed money to be able to keep her three-year-old daughter from being sent to an awful orphanage. I also think that she worked as a prostitute, I am not sure though. I didn't want to ask.

'Thanks Lilian, that's just what I was missing to bind the powder for the coral-coloured shade,' I told her.

'No problem, it's my job. I have to do it, there isn't much of a choice here,' Lilian responded and then left. She always looked sad, and I felt so bad for her. Like most of the time her eyes had been full of water today like she was about to cry. I was unsure if it was the chemicals that let her eyes react like that or her emotions.

I went back to creating my eyeshadow. I made the last adjustments to the recipe and then made my way down the stairs to the other part of the factory where all the products were produced on a large scale. It was a big room, and the walls were so tall they seemed like they were toughing the sky. The few windows let in small amounts of light. I was surrounded by machines that were roaring and screeching. Left and right from me people hustled around, carrying supplies, operating the machines and packaging the products. Occasional you would hear a loud cough. The air down there smelt putrid, worse than the scent of smoke and damp cardboard in the entrance. It was a mixture of all the chemicals used in the products and the diesel that was needed to operate the machines. It probably also came from some sort of mould or mildew that grew down there. It was not very sanitary. I gave the recipe to Fergus. He was the one who supervised the production. He was a tall black man, approximately two meters tall. He had scars all over his face and looked very scary, however though he was one of the friendliest guys that worked there. I had figured that out the first days I had been staying in the bunker when I started working here. His past was one of the darkest though. I don't even want to think about it.

'Sis you did a quite impressive job on this one. Unfortunately, I know our boss never gonna show you any pride,' he said. He was smiling at me, and it gave me this welcome feeling like I was wanted here. He stretched out his hand and patted my shoulder in recognition.

'Well I can be proud of myself for at least developing a new recipe,' I responded.

There was not much in my life that I could pat myself on the back for anymore.

'By the way, the colour on this one is amazing,' he continued to compliment.

'Yes, the aniline I mixed in really makes the colour remarkable, almost like the original. Although, I don't wanna know what it does to the skin. On that note, please tell your people to be careful with the aniline because it is highly flammable and can ruin the lungs if it's inhaled,' I responded.

'Ok! Now go back to makin' more phenomenal recipes before our boss sees us talking and not workin' and don't worry, I'm gonna make sure they're careful with the aniline,' he added. With that job done, I staggered back upstairs to my lab. I almost tripped on my way up the stairs. I wished they would invest in an elevator. But that would not happen that would be an investment for the workers what was not a thing in this place.

At six o'clock, I made my way home. I lived about half a kilometre away from the factory and I needed to walk the whole way with my crutches. The ground was covered in pine needles, tree roots and stones which made it tricky to walk. My house, the factory and the bunker are situated in an eighty-hectare forest. The forest consists of mostly pine trees but there are also various berry bushes. I used to pick berries and make jam out of them, but since we started dumping the toxic fluids in the river that passes the factory, I stopped eating any kind of produce that grows in the soil surrounding the factory. Most of the plants don't even produce flowers or fruits anymore. Those chemicals also had an impact on the wildlife. The only animals I ever saw was the occasional raven, cockroach, rat or fly. I was relieved when I opened the door of my small house. The house kind of looked like a witch's house or something like that or something like that. I was not allowed to live in the city cause our boss wanted to keep our lives hidden, to protect us, he had said. Except, actually, it was to protect the factory and his illegal business. He basically forced us to stay here and most of us were frightened of the outcome of leaving. At least, I was one of the lucky ones that had their own place and didn't need to share an area, like most of the others. Well, the only lucky one. The majority of the other factory workers were housed in the big bunker underground. Approximately two hundred meters from the factory. As soon as you entered the bunker you would have to hold your breath because otherwise, if you weren't used to the smell, you probably would throw up. The smell came from all the fungus that was growing down there. There was no way for fresh air to get in and the people lived on top of each other, literally. Each of them only had a small bed to themselves and had to share everything else. I had to stay there the first week I had worked at the factory. But I was moved to the little house, for my own sake I like to have my peace and quiet. I was lucky to get it because I could not stand that week in the bunker. I almost thought of committing suicide. Well, I thought of it, not only almost. I had planned out every miniscule detail. It had not been the first time the thought of killing myself had struck me.

I got home, watched the news and ate my dinner. My favourite part of the day. Not much else to enjoy. Rice with carrots – plain but tasty. I guess. Not enough money for anything fancy. But I was better off than some people – my friends in prison, for example. I could not afford more so I guess I had to live with it. Well actually, that was just a tiny problem or maybe not one at all. There was not a problem with rice and carrots, not at all they were two perfect things created by nature. I should have taken it as a privilege to have food and a roof of my own over my head, unlike my friends in prison. Well, if I could call them my friends. Like what are real friends? What I consider, I don't have real, real friends anymore. I used to have some when I was living my nice life in New York. I think I could call them my ex-friends now, that was the right term I suppose. I had lost all of them due to what I did, or what Mike did. Maybe, I shouldn't have gotten them involved. That was not very fair. It wasn't fair but how should I have known? I had never imagined it ending up the way it did. I thought everything I was doing was form the good side and not the dark illegal side. I did not just ruin my own life but also theirs. Mike had changed me into a person I wasn't. A person I was not supposed to be. A person, I did not want to be nor expected to be. Some of my university friends were in prison now just cause I had asked them for a small favour. I don't even know if I can call it a favour, cause it was supposed to be something that should have benefited my friends and I. I thought it was going to be something memorable. I thought it was legitimate but actually Mike had laid a trap, for his benefit, not mine. To be honest, they were better off in prison than that bunker.

Why did I trust him? I should have known that he did not actually want a friendship. All he had wanted was to benefit from my kindness and vulnerability. And my trust in him as a person, a good person. He just wanted to be his selfish persona. Well, now I know better not to trust anyone. But one thing I will never understand is why I did not end up in prison along with the others. Why did he make it look like my friends were the only guilty ones in front of the court and make himself and I look innocent? But just when I thought I had left that chapter of my life behind me, I had received a letter from the police saying I was being accused of cooperating in illegal affairs. Which was actually true. Why had Mike betrayed me after so many years? Well, it wasn't that long, if he had saved me from prison before? Maybe, he had just wanted to torture me by giving me a taste of a perfect life again and then ruining everything for me, my career, my health, literally my life by sending me to prison years later. After I had gotten out of prison, the only job I could get was the one at his factory. Maybe, it had been his plan all along. Mike is the worst human being there is. Why was I still under his control? He had taken everything he could from me. All I was left with was my soul and even that was not entirely mine. He had taken my identity, like literally he had taken my ID, my papers everything that made me a valid human on this modern planet.

'I should stand up and tell the police everything. I have evidence but he would probably turn it against me again. But who cares? I have a shitty life anyway I have nothing to lose, except maybe my life. But I am strong now, I could save myself, I could be a hero,' I said out loud as I took another spoonful of rice. A few grains fell down on the floor and I kicked them under the table. I was filled with eagerness to diminish this person I called Mike. He had no right to make me so small. He was not something better he was something worse. I put down my one foot down on the blue carped floor with all the force I had and made my way to the kitchen. I was filled with energy, I felt better than I had in a long time. I was strong, independent and free. I could be free. I could take my life back, he could not hold me back from that, I was way too valuable to be thrown away like that. I had worth; he just had made me blind to see it. But I had just ripped the sunglasses from my damaged face, I saw the reality. I stroke the maple of the wooden kitchen table. It was kind of falling apart. It had probably been left in the sun or something. The laker was peeling off and the sheer touch made me feel the splinters entering into my hand. But it felt more real than anything had in a long time.

The next day I took a chance I did not go to that stupid factory, I walked to the nearest road and hitchhiked to the city. I don't know what had gotten into me. I don't know what I had gotten myself into. I felt so badass doing this. I was as full of courage like the last time when I had left this rancid place. It was kind of scary and I was robbed on the way. I didn't' really lose anything valuable except ten bucks. Which I didn't really care about. But I had gotten to the city, oh how I had missed New York. I felt the wind blowing through my long brown hair. I practically ran to the police station. I felt free. When I was working for Mike, I had felt more captured than when I was in prison. Prison was captivity for my body but not for my mind. I still had hope back then. Being trapped at the factory was like being in a cell without my soul. It was like I did not even exist. I looked down to the ground and watched my blue and pink running shoes move on the broken pavement, occasionally I would see a small weed climbing up between the cracks. I related to those plants, I was just like them. I swung the big glass police door open. I felt so euphoric. I could not believe how many people were sitting there. But I did not mind waiting. I was safe here. And I had wasted most of my life on Mike, the best years of my life. These minutes would not be wasted for him but against him. It smelled so clean in the police station. Everything was so sterile in comparison to the factory. The full police office was filled with blue armrest chairs and some green plants. I scanned the people's faces in the waiting room, I saw people of all shapes and sizes. Literally there were small people, there were tall people, there were skinny people, there were fat people, there were old and young people. A little boy wearing a green cap caught my attention. He was sitting on his mother's lap crying. He had a bleeding knee but other than that he looked good and healthy. His handy were tiny and were holding a play truck which was still covered in sand. When I looked closer, I could see the sand on his white socks and on his stripped blue shorts. I sat down in one of the last free chairs. It felt so good. I had not sat in such a comfortable chair in a long time. The last time had been in the court waiting room before I was taken to the women's prison in west Virginia. That was the second time I had been to court. The first time was when I had been declared innocent and my university friends were sent to prison forever. Lifelong sentences. Honestly, this would never stop confusing me.

There was an old lady sitting next to me. We had a small conversation, in which I pretended to be a normal person with a normal life. I could not tell this lady about my catastrophic life. She looked so delicate she probably would have had a heart attack if I would have told her the truth. I should not even be thinking about the consequences of telling her the truth. This was typical me again though, lying. I would never have done that before I met Mike.

But when the old lady – Elizabeth – asked, 'So why are you here?', I was shocked and did not know what to say. I was totally taken off guard. I was unprepared for that question even though it was an obvious one. I had not thought things through, I did not think I was going to have to have a conversation with anyone. My brain had not gotten that far yet.

I quickly answered, 'I want to tell the police something they need to know.'

Elizabeth must have been a wise lady, or she just did not care and said, 'Don't worry you don't need to tell me. She had a smirk on her face as if she was amused by my answer. Personally, I don't wanna tell you either why I am her, but since I can't keep my mouth shut, I will tell you ...'

I was so stunned after she had told me her whole story. With every letter she used to tell me her story I saw different wrinkles forming in her face. I felt connected with her. We were soulmates. Our conversation progressed for hours as we waited for our turn to talk to the police. She had told me that she had been working in prostitution for years and got dragged into the drug business. I had not expected that from her at all. She was this adorable old lady that could be working in a library. She had been raped by the owner of the brothel, accused of stealing their and been used her whole life. She told me about how she always was searching the meaning in life but simply could not find it. Even though she went through a lot and basically lived a wasted life she seemed happy and did not seem to mind the course of her life, it did not seem to bother her. She went on telling me about the love of her life, who had been a Jew. As she was Muslim she had run away from home for him. Times changed and they fell out of love. She said the cultural and spiritual barrier was too big and left them fighting. She told me about how he had abused her for years before she finally left him. She was left alone with a child with nothing else than a suitcase with clothes and a mind filled with depressed thoughts. Her son overdosed and died tragically. She ended up in a brothel, later in prison for robbery and now she was here. Over the years she had gotten out of prostituting, because she was to old and as she put it too ugly, but she had stayed in the drug business. She was an excellent mule, who expected an old lady to be carrying drugs. She had had a good or let's say ok relationship with her boss, however, lately he had forced her to swallow drugs again and she had had enough. She wanted to turn herself in so she could retire in prison. I don't know what I was supposed to think about that plan nor about the fact that she treated everything like a joke and made a huge story out of everything but well she was keeping my mind off of the obvious. In the end I told her my story. But I should have learned not to trust anybody. But I could not resist telling her this. It felt like an obligation in me, I could not hold my secrets within me anymore. I felt like I was doing it against my own will. I had lost control of what I was thinking and I was unable to restrain the words coming out of my mouth.

After I had told her my story, she said, 'Be careful.' And looked at me with an expression that wanted to say a thousand words but couldn't. Was she somehow connected, or had I just met a crazy lady?

It was Elisabeth's turn to go into the police office. But after she had entered the room, she never came back. The wooden doors of the office stayed close and did not swing open every few minutes like the had before. I did not figure anything bad, but I should have. I was called in to the office. But oddly I was taken back out with a police officer without even being able to say a single word. I was brought into an alleyway behind the police station. But I was just told to follow and that's what I had done. Dumb me once again. The policeman that was leading me outside the station had told me his name was Daniel. He was tall and skinny; his face was round and he had short brown hair. He frightened me because his mood had turned as soon as we had left the station. His face was filled with emotions I could not figure out. He looked scared but at the same time he frightened me. He had aggressively grabbed me and pulled me into a dark alley that was about a block away from the police station. I hated these places in New York. They had always seemed scary to me especially after I had worked with Mike, and I had seen what he did there. My mind was turning rapidly. I had so many flashbacks to terrible things that had happened to me and to other people. I could remember myself standing in an alley about thirteen years ago. My tiny body had been trembling with fear and anxiety. But when my perfectly red-lacquered fingernails had passed through my then still soft brown hair, I remembered it was not me that had to be afraid. It was my friends that were not worth anything anymore to Mike. My mind got interrupted by a very angry voice. This time I should have trembled with fear, but I didn't. I looked down at my know dirty nails and ripped skin. My hands were filled with scars and didn't look nice and kept like they used to. But they were still they were calm, I was not afraid. All my anxiety had faded, if I just knew why.

'Mia you are such an unroyal Bitch! I gave you a job after you left prison. I gave you a place to live and now you want to turn me in. Well, you should have thought twice about doing that. I don't go to prison, other people do.'

I saw Mike's face in the darkness of the alleyway. I was astounded. I had not seen his face in forever or that is at least what it felt like. I wanted to hit him so badly. Tell him what I thought of him. I felt my hands forming fists. But before I had more of those thoughts, I saw Elizabeth covered in blood lying on the floor. Her face was pale, and she looked, I don't know, I don't even want to know. Her grey hair was stuck together with blood. Her cute little dress was torn in pieces. I could smell the fresh blood mixed with the stink of garbage which was piled in a bin at the end of the alley. Her mouth was open and her eyes rolled back.

'You don't even have anything to say you little traitor,' Mike yelled me.

I did. I had so much to say but no words could be formed in my mouth. My lips felt frozen. It was all so surreal. He looked straight at me, staring straight into my brown eyes. I felt like he was trying to destroy me by simply looking at me. I could not think straight, I was empty. No, that was not the right word. I was looking deep into Mikes eyes, and I felt like I was sinking into them. I felt something cold and pointy stab my back. It hurt but it felt nice, I was enjoying the pain. What was wrong with me, I was enjoying being killed? Did I really hate myself that much, that it gave me pleasure to fade away from this planet? I heard Mike laugh, his mean nasty laugh. It definitely brought him joy hurting others. Therefore, I enjoyed the 'pain' even more. Because if he enjoyed hurting people and I did not let him hurt me, I was kind of taking his joy. I did not even try to resist the force of the thing he was stabbing into me. It felt good. He had taken so much happiness from me. I could take some of his, even though I could not let him know and he probably would never know. I did not care. I was never going to need to deal with him again, never. So, I thought. It was over, all my agony would end now. It was finally over.

UNWANTED SECOND CHANCES

My eyelids slowly opened and adjusted to the light. I could feel my leg muscles slowly waking up. I regained the control over my movements. With time I could feel the weakness fade away and my body slowly reclaiming strength. I woke up, it did not feel different from other times I woke up. Maybe I was just a bit more in pain than normal. I was in some room. It was cool and it smelled really clean, like disinfectant. But I was petrified. This place gave me a weird vibe. This was not heaven. Wait, didn't I just die? It could not be hell. I wondered if this is how it felt after you died, I could not feel like this. I don't think it should feel this normal. Death should be something you have never experienced before. But I felt like I was waking up to a normal day. I sat up and stared at the light blue wall. I turned my head and looked through a window. On a door in the distance, I read 'North Psychiatric Institution' written in big bold yellow letters. What had happened? Why didn't he kill me? Did he know I was enjoying my 'death'? Who was this person I called Mike? How well did he know me? Was he afraid to lose me, for whatever reason or did he want me to have a nightmare life without an end? Maybe all of this was just a bad dream I was going to wake up from any moment. I could at least hope. But nothing made sense. The questions were running through my head like a waterfall. They would not stop. When I turned my head further, I saw him lying next to me. His arms and legs were tied down to a small bed. My mouth fell open and I got a weird feeling. We were both in a psychiatry. And I was not even close to being a hero. Who was I? My thoughts in my head were twisting and turning in all possible directions. Nothing was making sense anymore. I was so confused. I am literally a confusion. I was not even sure if this was all real or it was just a dream. I felt someone pinching my shoulder. I turned to see who it was. After me awkwardly staring in their eyes I realized it was a nurse who had come into the room without me even noticing her. She was wearing a white cote and white pants and those weird white crock kind of shoes. After she acknowledged that she had gotten my attention she gave me a huge friendly smile. Her face was a bit tanned which contrasted her very white outfit.

'How are you feeling?', she asked.

Without even thinking I just answered; 'ok.'

But I was not feeling ok, ok. I was feeling the opposite of ok. Was it ok not to be feeling ok? What does it mean to be ok? Before I lost myself even more in my thoughts, which happens very frequently the nurse said, 'That's good to hear. My name is Allyssa, and I will be taking care of you.'

So, wait a second, was I that unstable that I needed an 'Allyssa' to take care of me? All I wanted was to get out of this place. I did not want to be here. Like why would I? Mike was here, I apparently needed care, it was unfamiliar, and I didn't even have enough room to think about anymore good arguments.

'Would you like to tell me your name?', Allyssa continued.

'I am Mia David, and what on earth am I doing here? I don't want to be here', I replied in a very loud, irritated voice. I was mad. I did not want to be here. Better dead than here.

I think Allyssa heard my anger. I guess her strokes along my back should have been soothing or something like that. But they weren't, I did not like it when people touched me. 'Stop you bitch!', I yelled.

Allyssa was clearly shocked and immediately pulled her hand away and said, 'Frist of all, you are here as a patient and cannot leave till you are in a stable condition. Second, you have no right to be mean to me or the other nurses, cause all they want to do is help you by doing their job. And last but not least maybe you don't want to be here now but trust me being here will help you in the future. I am used to dealing with people like you.' Like me, what was that supposed to mean? I was not mental, I was perfectly fine. Better I would be if they just let me get out of this horrendous place. I felt like I was being treated like a child.

Alyssa continued her speech. 'In one hour, you have an appointment with our trauma doctor. Till then I will show you around the facilities and explain all the rules to you. So, could you please follow me?'

I stood up to follow this bitchy nurse. Although most people would have preserved her as kind and friendly to me she wasn't. I already did not like her. I was not going to like anyone here.

'What about Mike?' I yelled.

I was so mad, I just did not understand what was happening and I wanted to so badly. I had thought that everything was over that I never would need to suffer again but it wasn't. The situation was maybe even worse than before. Insult added to injury, as my mom would have said.

Allyssa answered, 'Oh, he is in a very critical condition. I am not allowed to unstrap him before he calms down. Because otherwise he could become violent with the other patients again. And we don't want that do we? Normally violent and aggressive patients are put into single rooms where the doors are locked at all times. Unfortunately, those rooms are all full at the moment and the only vacant bed was the one in your room. And since you two know each other, we thought it would be nice for both of you to have some company.'

Without hesitation I roared; 'Mike is not welcome company.'

'I think we will start with the rules before I show you around. Because you just broke one for the second time. There is no shouting allowed. Please try to keep your voice down'

I lost her after that rule. My mind was too occupied to be actually listening to her. I just did not understand. We walked out of the small room where Mike was still strapped to the bed. Apart from the door with the small window there was a mirror with a little sink under it that I had not noticed before. Beside each bed little tables with lamps were placed. I also noted that someone had drawn cigarettes on the wall or something that resembled a cigarette, as me and Alyssa exited the room through the door which was right beside the sink.

She said, 'On your left you can see the bathrooms and showers which you will be able to use between eight and nine o'clock. You're not allowed to use the showers or toilets further down the hall, they are only for our male patients.'

I was so tempted to ask: What if I am Transgender, which shower can I use. But I held back. I continued following her. She showed me the different sections of the psychiatry. Every section had two bathrooms, one for the female patients and one for the male patients. Moreover, every section had a doctor's office and a room for the nurses. Apparently, every section was for a certain kind of mental illness or disorder or whatever. Me and Mike had landed in the section for patients who had experienced traumatizing events. Allyssa had explained a lot of rules: I was not allowed to yell, run nor talk to other patients in the hallways. Neither was I allowed to be in the other sections without a nurse or doctor by my side. There were also set times when I was allowed to be somewhere and what I was allowed to do in that time. I was not too bothered by the rules. if I broke them maybe I would be kicked out and that would be a good thing in my opinion.

Finally, we had seen all the sections and Allyssa showed me the big canteen where all meals where served. It smelled like someone was making fresh bread. Gosh, how I could go for a nice warm slice of bread right now. Outside of the cafeteria there was a big park with benches and trees. Allyssa had told me that I could be outside without a nurse or a doctor as soon as I started to become more stable. Overall, the psychiatry hospital had really nice facilities. But that did not change my opinion. I still did not wanna be here. There was no need for me to be here. I continued following Allyssa across the grounds of the psychiatry till we got back to Mike's and my room. As we entered the small room, I saw that Mike was no longer inside, no longer was he strapped down to the bed. I was relieved that we had finally finished walking around, my leg was exhausted, and my shoulders were aching due to the crutches I had been using. Allyssa told me to change into white track pants and a white polo shirt which had been placed on my bed and wait for someone to bring me to the doctor's office. I took off my plain jeans and basic t-shirt, which was full of holes and stains due to acid that I used to make certain hair dies, well and also all the other chemicals. Allyssa gestured me to place my clothes in a bucket she was holding towards me.

'You will get them back when you have recovered and leave,' she said.

At this point I did not care what was happening to my torn clothes. They were trash anyhow. The track pants were fine, but the shirt was ass weird. Like it did not fit properly nor was it comfortable. It also made me look like I had a huge upper body which was not the case. A little bit later a doctor, who called himself Dr. Splean, came in.

'Please follow me into my office,' Splean said in a doctosrish voice. Why was he like this, he clearly thought he was superior to human kind.

I stood up and followed him down the hall. His office was furnished with an examination table, a desk and three chairs as well as a few cupboards and a sink. I sat my fat ass on the comfy chair beside his desk. I just did not get why I was here? How had this all happened? Since when did someone just wake up in a psychiatry hospital?

The doctor sat across from me and started staring at me as if he did not know what to do. After what felt like an eternity he asked; 'So do you remember anything that happened last night?'

Wait, what was last night? I could remember being at the police office but was that yesterday or was that a long time ago? How the hell should I be capable of knowing that? I had not even questioned how I had gotten to the psychiatric hospital yet. How had I not thought of that yet? Like, had they just picked me up on the street and thought this lady looks mental, let's stick her in a mental institution? I just did not understand. It was like I was a doll that someone was playing with. I don't un-

22

derstand. Usually, I would blame Mike for stuff like this, but since he was in here with me probably didn't bring me here. Or did he? He was so unpredictable. I just wanted to wake and realise its all a dream.

'What day was it yesterday?' I asked.

Dr. Splean answered, 'The 16th of July.'

Well, I guess I should have expected that. How on earth was a number going to help me figure out if yesterday was the yesterday, I thought it was?

So, I simply replied, 'Not really, can you tell me what happened?'

He frowned and started babbling. 'So, we don't know exactly either, but you and a young man were found in an alleyway both lying on the pavement. Beside you there was a pool of blood in which a dead body of an about 80-year-old lady lay. You and the young man were rushed to the hospital, thankfully you only just had some traces of GHB (4-Hydroxybutanoic acid) in your blood. After your check-up was finished at the hospital you were brought here to recover. The police are running investigations and think that you and Mike were witnesses to a murder. That is why you are here, because we think you are suffering a trauma and have lost your memory due to that traumatic event.'

So yesterday was the yesterday I thought it was.

'How long will I have to stay here?', I asked.

He answered exactly as I expected, 'Until you are in a stable mental condition.'

This guy frustrated me; 'What is a stable mental condition and how can I be traumatized by something I apparently don't remember? And when will I be in a stable condition?'

'When you are. Some patients take longer than others. It is just like that; you would not understand more details, you are not a doctor. You just have to accept it the way it is,' he replied.

He was such a lazy doctor. Like omg can you not just tell me, is your time that limited? Am I sooo stupid that I am not able to understand the definition of a stable mental condition? And to be honest I would understand because most of the things that happen in the brain have to do with chemistry and I understand that pretty well. I think Mr. Splean was daydreaming for quite some time, cause he just stared at the celling and spun around in his office chair. I was laughing inwardly because every couple of turns he would hit his legs on his glass desk. I hoped that he would get a horrible bruise there. Then I think he noticed me in the corner of his eye and suddenly stooped. He probably was pretty embarrassed because he started sweating really badly and got amazing looking sweat marks under his arms. Those would be hard stains to get out of his button-down shirt. Baking soda would probably help. His face turned red like a tomato. He then continued his examination or whatever we want to call it. I was told to lay down on the bed. Then he started tapping and touching my head. I was not exactly sure how he should determine my apparent trauma through that. I thought I would leave this place with a trauma from him. After he finished bruising my head with his rock-hard hands, he said that he wanted to do a brain scan. I followed him to another section of the psychiatry hospital where there were machines everywhere. He told me that this used to be the section for trauma patients but after renovation they had made it a surgery room as well as rooms for x-rays and PET-scans and other scanning things I had never heard about. He sounded so proud when he was talking about all of it, like he was proving his intelligence. Or like this place belonged to him. But the majority of what he was saying did not matter to me. Apparently, the section where trauma patients were now used to be for patients with addictions. That would explain the cigarette drawings on the wall or maybe it was marihuana or some other drug. The scan was over relatively quickly, he made me take off all my clothes including my bra. He had told me that I cannot have anything metallic on me and my bra could contain metal. I was not dumb a sports bra did not have metal it was not one with metal but whatever. I got in this futuristic tube and sound were coming from everywhere going through every part of my body. Leaving me there full of unhealthy radiation. We went back the trauma section of the psychiatry. This time we passed a lot of patients. And honestly, they were all super weird. Some of them were talking to themselves, some of them were twitching, one younger woman I passed was constantly hitting herself in the head and had a huge bruise due to that. Or that's at least what I thought. When we arrived back, he told me we were done for today and that I could go have dinner now and then go to my room. Mike was still nowhere to be seen. I had walked too much that day, for sure. My shoulders were about to fall off and even my wrist had stared to ache. But I was starving. I probably had not eaten anything in two days. The last thing I had was rice with carrots, I remember. I made my way back to the canteen, it smelt so damn good the water in my mouth started to run and my stomach started to grumble even more. There was a big electronic menu at the front. I was so hungry; I did not even take the time to read it. I just walked as fast as I could with the crutches to the canteen counter where food was been given out. I just asked the anorexic looking teenage girl to give me whatever she recommended. She looked at me and turned her head to the side.

'So, wait a second you are asking me, who dreads eating anything, what you should eat. I am sorry that is kind of a hard question to answer. But honestly, take the pasta. It looks the best.'

She gave me the pasta and I was off to find a table where no one else was sitting. I found one at the end of the cafeteria beside the big glass doors, through which you could see the garden. I sat down and started to devour my food. My eyes saw nothing more than my plate in front of me. I had gone in to tunnel vision. I was in my own world and there was no way someone was going to disturb me. I was stuffing enormous mouthfuls down my trough. Pasta had never tasted this good. Well, I did not care what it tasted like at that moment. I was soo focused on eating, that I must have missed the moment that the anorexic girl, sat down across from me. She was definitely watching me eat. And certainty judging me. But what did I care? When I finished my plate, I looked up. She had a beautiful face, and her hair was astounding. It was extremely long and fell beautifully over her shoulders. It had this fascinating natural shape that the curls kept in place. When the sun hit her head, it was reflected back. But she did not look healthy at all: Her arms were just two bones and the trackpants were so loose on her that it looked like she was wearing more of a skirt than pants. Her collarbones were sticking out of her skin so much that it looked like they were going to break through the skin any moment. It looked painful and gave me goosebumps all over my skin. And under her eyes two black rings had formed which looked quite dramatic in contrast to her pale face. Her arms were tiny and the shirt holes were gigantic compared to them. I looked down on the table and saw her hand, I got the shivers by the look of it. I just saw her body crumbling down in my inner eye.

'I have never seen someone eat their food that fast,' she said pointedly.

'I was just starving,' I replied.

I just hoped I would be cold enough that she would leave me alone and go about her own business. I could not deal with another person right now. I needed space. I did not want to talk to her I just wanted to be left alone, I wanted to be lonely more than being aggravated by this teenage girl. I looked over at her plate. All that was there was where three pieces of broccoli and half a potato. She sat down across from me, and she just started shoved the food around her plate. She did not even try to eat it. Or at least that is what I thought. What I was seeing. We just sat in silence. And for some reason I did not mind her company very much. Not as much as I had expected. I don't know what it was about her, but she gave me the same vibes that the old lady had given me. And that was a rare feeling, well not so rare lately. I did not feel comfortable with many people anymore. I felt so bad for the old lady – why did Mike need to kill her, or better said why did he need to command someone to kill her? What had she done, what had she known? I went back to her past in my mind, and it had nothing to do with Mike. She had told me how she had been abused by her husband for years. How he had been violent towards her. But nothing in relation to Mike. She had told me about how she thought of killing herself to escape. To just get rid of the emotions that were killing her from the inside. It was the drugs for sure. Ugh why was she involved in drugs. If you were involved with drugs you were involved with Mike. Why did he need to be like this?

'I am Alice by the way, what's your name?' She asked.

'I am Mia.'

'I don't know if you are allowed, but you could ask your nurse if we could go out in the park tomorrow, if you want. I am really bored here, and I can't stand most of the patients. But you seem to be more normal and no freako like the others.'

Why did I like this girl soo much, it seemed like we had been friends for a long time. How could she have managed to figure out in such a short time that I was not like the others here. Did I make such a good first impression? She had a sassy attitude which I liked. Plus, maybe it would make me seem more stable if I made friends. Or something like that. So, I agreed to ask my nurse tomorrow. After I put away my tray I went back to my room. I was afraid of opening the door cause I didn't know if Mike would be there. But as I peeked through the door he was nowhere to be seen. I let out a sigh of relief. So, I plunked myself on my bed. I woke up because I felt something on my forehead. There was disinfectant being sprayed from automatic sprayers all around the room. It smelt bad but not horrible. It reminded me of dentist visits a long time ago when I had to get my wisdom teeth pulled. That was a horrible experience back then but if I think back now it was nothing compared to what happens to you when you get involved in illegal things; in counterfeiting. As I lay in my bed and inhaled the smell of cleanness, I felt all the pain I had in my one leg and stump, as well as my arms I was all cramped up. But the more I could relax the more the pain faded. I also started to remember my dream from that night. Or at least parts of it. I remembered a part where I got picked up by an ambulance and another where Mike was choking. But I could not make much out of that. I turned my head. Mike was still not in sight. I felt liberated. Thank God. The door creaked and Allyssa came walking in with a clipboard and a pen.

'Checks.'

Again, she was smiling. I think she was someone who was always happy. Maybe that's why she was so unsympathetic to me. Maybe that's why in my mind she was a bitch. She sat down at the end of my bed and asked:

'How are you doing?'

'Ok, are you going to ask me that every day or will I one day not need to answer the exact same question?'

'I am obligated to ask how you are doing on every given day. But you only need to give me a simple answer and nothing more. If you want of course, you can give me a detailed description. But somehow, I think you are never going to want to do that.'

I remembered to ask, 'Since I am not allowed to leave this place, am I allowed to go out with Alice today?'

She replied, 'Depends if you cooperate in your therapy session today, but if you do, I could possibly let you go.', she smiled at me, she seemed presently surprised by the news.

Was this lady serious? First, I need to go to a doctor's appointment and get scans and now I need to go to therapy? But somehow, I was in a good mood that day and decided to go with the flow. It would probably be the fastest way to get out of there. I could stop trying to fight the system for once. I could just take a break.

MEXICO CITY

After what felt like waiting for Christmas as a child a male carer came in to take me to therapy. I followed everything he said and did not even complain once. Just maybe because I cooperated and was nice for once I did not need to take the stairs to the upper level of the building but instead, I was allowed to take the elevator. I was so glad, that saved me some pain and probably an embarrassing fall. It really did not matter how many times I climbed stairs; I would fall for sure half of the time. He led me into a room which had walls covered in pictures of nature. In the middle there were like one million pillows and an around 75-year-old man sitting and meditating. The carer told me to sit down and relax. He left. As soon as the old man heard the door close, he opened his eyes. And looked at me with a smile. Why did everyone smile here. Could they just look at me normally.

'Please lie down and just try to remember what happened.'

I did as I was told, except I did not really try remembering. I just pretended to.

'Now take a deep breath in and then exhale, exhale all the bad memories that are stuck inside of you.'

This dude was definitely supposed to be some voodoo slash yoga slash hippy guy.

'Inhale and exhale.'

This went on forever but then he finally said that I could sit up. He told me I should do it every day in order to calm myself and reduce the anxiety and stress caused by the trauma. I thought we were done but I was wrong. Now he wanted me to sit down and tell him what I felt inside when I saw different patterns which were drawn on paper in different colors. They just looked like drawings a four-year-old did in preschool. But since

I promised to do what I was told, I tried to say something that somehow made some sense.

'I feel pain inside of me that I can not let go.'

I felt ridiculous doing this. I was lying again, just making up stories. Sometimes it felt like I lived in my lies for so long that they seemed real to me.

'Inhale and exhale, just clean your soul from the bad things that have happened in your life.' This went on for like ten drawings till the last one came which was kind of a line that resembled the shape of a eyeliner. Well, it basically was a line on a paper, but eyeliner just popped in my mind.

'Eyeliner.'

'What?' he responded, with a confused expression.

I did not want to say that out loud, so much for control.

'I just said that cause I just remembered that I did not put any eyeliner on this morning. I actually wanted to say that it reminds me of a wound which is dripping blood.'

What the hell had I just said? I never use eyeliner. Well, I have used it once or twice in my life but still. The voodoo man just gave me another look of puzzlement, he looked soo odd with his white beard and his wrinkled forehead. What kind of psychiatry was this? I don't think this kind of therapy is medically proven.

'I think we are done for today.'

I was taken back to my room by the same carer as before. As we passed another section of the psychiatric hospital, I spotted Mike followed by two carers and a nurse. He did not look like himself. He looked like a body without a soul. He was empty. He looked like he had no energy and that spark in his eyes that he had before was missing. But before I could get a better look he disappeared into an elevator. I made it back to my room and on the door there was a note hanging.

Mia; you may go out with Alice before lunch for one hour. That means from eleven to twelve.

Allyssa

I got pretty excited. Maybe me and Alice could become friends But that was not a good idea cause I know what happens to people who become my friends. And I didn't want that for her I didn't want to bring misery over her. I didn't want her to end up in jail. I heard a knock on my door and when I saw Alice through the metal bars that covered the small window on the door, I was thrilled. We made our way outside in silence. When we were outside the silence started to become awkward. I tried to find something to say. It felt weird since I did not know her one bit and we did not have much in common so far, apart from us both being in a psychiatric institution. On top of that the age gap scared me. I could be her mother. It just gave me a weird vibe. I started thinking this was a bad idea and started regretting my life decisions.

'So I suppose you're in the section for addiction?', I asked.

Now that was a weird question to ask but just as sassy as she was, she replied, 'Of course, I am addicted to starving myself and to seeing the number drop on the scale. Look at me. I know that you are here because of a trauma, but what traumatised you?'

How was I supposed to answer that question? 'I don't know exactly because I don't think I am suffering from a trauma.'

'This place is weird, maybe we should just pretend we are normal people and not talk about this place or anything that has to do with it,' she said.

I felt like I was being younger than I was. I felt like I had even acted like a child previously. Can I even pretend to be a normal person because I am probably the opposite of normal? Well, but pretending was always something I was kind of good at. Lying was another specialty of mine. Well at least till a certain point where everything I pretended just busted and everything came up, all the lies, all the things that were fake and pretended. It always ends in a bad way. But will I learn from those mistakes. Probably not. Actually, no I won't. I got no energy to be a fully honest person. And being honest can sometimes also lead to pain and I don't need nor want that pain.

'How old are you?' I asked.

31

'I just turned 18 a while ago, I know I just said a few seconds ago that maybe we shouldn't talk about this place or things that have to do with it and maybe it doesn't have anything to do with it, but I like knowing things and I have been wondering since yesterday why you are missing one leg. What's the story?'

Truth or lie. What was I supposed to do? Well, what was I supposed to say? I didn't want what happened to Elisabeth to happen to her if I told her the truth.

So, 'I was born without it.' I said quickly.

'I know you are lying, tell me the truth, you can't keep it from me now. And remember I give out the food so I could easily let you starve.', she said and gave me a chickee smile.

She was a really sassy girl. I did not want to tell her. I had no desire to go back into those memories. She was anyhow just bluffing with starving me. Like she had nothing to hold against me, nothing she could pressure me with. 'But what if the truth kills you.' It was good that we were walking alone along the cobbled stone path in the park because this way there was no one near us who could overhear our conversation. Excluding the chirping birds in the trees. What did I have to lose? Well, a lot but did I care. Not exactly. Or was I lying to myself again? I did not know. I could not make my mind up about it.

'Look at me I am a walking skeleton and close to die anyway so just tell me, I am good at keeping my mouth shut. I probably will starve myself before your truth kills me.'

I replied with sincerity:' But I don't want you to die.'

She looked at me as if she wanted to tell me there was no need to worry:

'That's a lot of feelings in one sentence for not knowing each other very long. I have a marvelous idea; so, everyday we go out into the park, you tell me about whatever led to you losing one leg and at dinner you are allowed to make me eat something to keep me alive until I know the whole story. Then I might die of your truth instead of starvation. I think that would be a more interesting death. Something people could talk about. It would probably also be better for my family since they would not blame my death or their upbringing and on my condition.'

She looked at me with a huge smile. This deal was stupid, I felt like I was in middle school doing bets and deals. But what was I supposed to do anyway? I had nothing better to do. I was going to be bored here anyway. And I really wanted her to get better. She still had so much of life left and soo much that she could do without a criminal record with a valid passport as a valid person. Well, at least I didn't think had a criminal record. Her mind was still intact, their was just a small default with her eating disorder, however, that could be fixed unlike my problems.

'Well, I will agree to the deal as you call it, if you eat something every dinner even when I have finished telling my story.'

'Sealed!' she yelled out into the garden and grabbed my hand to shake it firmly. She took it in a way like big businessmen do, squeezing the palm with the right and kind of tapping the back of the hand with the left. As she shook it I could feel every bone in her hand, I was afraid it was going to just crumble. A few people in the garden must have heard cause they had turned to look at us. Soon after they lost interest and went back to whatever they were doing.

'But it starts tomorrow cause we need to be back in exactly 13 min,' I told her. I did not wanna mess with Alyssa today. I was following the system. Instead of going to eat lunch Alice disappeared. Alice reminded me of my times in high school. I think the way I was today I probably was behaving ten or twelve years younger than I was. Or more. I don't now if Alice realized that I was soo much older than she was. Maybe she just didn't care. Maybe I just looked young. I don't think so. But maybe she had a different perception. Well, age was just a number, maybe she was desperately lonely. She was actually, she had admitted it I think.

'Hey Mia!', was the first thing I heard upon entering my room.

When I saw Mike, I took a step back. How immeasurably I hated him. I felt the muscles in my face become tense, I started to feel unwell. His presence started to turn my stomach upside down.

'Its all your fault that I have ended up here!' He started cursing at me. He looked me straight in the eyes just staring, he did not even wink once. I leaned back to increase the distance between us.

He insulted me once more. I think he was so loud that the nurses must have heard him and before he was able to touch me nurses, carers and doctors had rushed in and pulled him out of the room. It felt so overwhelming cause I was not used to getting attention like this. They grabbed him by his arms and dragged them out. He tried to fight back, but they were outnumbered by far. I would have loved to have screamed: untouchable, soo untouchable. Mike belonged here; he definitely was not good nor ok nor stable mentally. He was dangerous, mean, horrible, disgusting and every other word that had somewhat to do with something bad; he was hell. The only good thing about him were his eyes. They just were amazing. However, I wish I could rip them out, I did not want to look at them anymore. I did not want to be sickened by them anymore. Alyssa came rushing in to calm me down, but I was calm. This was how Mike normally behaved. She wanted to try to calm me by stroking my back, but I had already told her once that I don't like that, so I yelled, 'Don't you remember!'

Bitch. I think she got a bit offended and left the room, but I did not mind cause I finally had my peace and quiet. But then I started thinking of what would happen to the factory if Mike was here. Was everything still running? Or did everything shut down? Did some employee's aka slaves flee or did maybe even the police figure out something? Just imagine if I managed to give them a hint to shut down Mike's illegal business. Then I could call myself a hero. Then I would be happy that Mike did not kill me, cause if his business got uncovered, he would need to go to jail and therefore fail in his life goal. I would see him suffering for a change. I would see him get what he deserved. I felt warm inside just thinking of it. Was I becoming like Mike? Why was I full of joy when thinking of the harm that would be done to him, or that could be done to him? Was I a horrible person? Maybe I was just like Mike. NO. No way, there was no way. I should not compare myself to him, I was soo much better. I was an angel compared to him. I thought I had stopped comparing myself to him. The rest of the day I spent staring at the cigarette drawings on the wall while lying in bed. I couldn't find any motivation. Not for anything really. I was just daydreaming of how my story would end and how I would spend the rest of my life. Would I ever manage to get a real job with my criminal record, without an ID? To society I was just like nonexistent. Most likely not. But anyway, my only life goal is to take Mike down now. Maybe if I could help the police uncover his illegal businesses, they could do something about my criminal record or my passport and ID that have gone missing. Well, are in Mike's possession. Or maybe they would give me a reward which would be enough to live off. I would just need to hope for the best. And hope dies last. And if it does not, I can still commit suicide. No one can stop me from that except myself. But that would not fulfill my new life goal, so it is only plan B. I was again awakened when I felt cold drops of disinfectant attacking my face. They were literally attacking my face and when they ended up in my eyes it burned like hell. The drop would hit my face and it would begin to burn the pain would spread and then eventually fade but, in the meantime, a new drop would land on my face again and the story would start again. Why did they need to spray disinfectant, like its not like I am that unhygienic. I must have slept for a pretty long time because since the incident with Mike I had been in bed. Did it matter? Not the tiniest bit. I decided I was going to go for a shower. I had not showered since I had gotten here. It was probably about time. After I finished, I changed back into the weird ass white outfit. I went back into my room, which I probably had to myself now. What was I supposed to do the whole day? I know that Alice would want to go out, but did I want to? I was afraid; I did not want to get attached to her. As fate would have it, when I finished eating breakfast Alice caught me in the hallway. I was dreading talking to her. I did not want to tell her the truth. It was too dark. To disturbing, I could not even handle it myself. I was not over what had happened. I was still full of regret, and I did not want those feeling to come back. I wanted to keep them as far away as possible I never wanted to open that drawer in my head. It was locked and never to be opened. I had taken the key and sunk it in my pool of emotions in my head, it was so big and such a mess that no one could find it there that was for sure.

'Good morning, Mia. I am impatiently waiting for your story.'

Ugh. She remembered. Well of course she did. What was I expecting? There was not that much happening here so that she would just totally forget she had ever seen me. She was not insane, for as much as that counts.

'Meet you in the park at four, after my weigh-in appointment.'

Ugh. Why? She was not asking me but telling me. It seemed like she was certain I wanted to tell her about my whole life. I did like her, but this was not going to end well. I had destroyed a lot of people's lives, I didn't want to make hers even worse. I did not want to like her, I was going to have to find a way to dislike her. There was no other way.

'OK,' I muttered.

I continued on my way to my room where I was planning to do some daydreaming. I loved daydreaming; it was so calming. Just losing myself in my thoughts. Well, it was calming till I started stressing or thinking about all the bad stuff that I had done or the horrible things that had happened to me or if I thought about how my current disastrous life looks.

'Mia, you have to go to Dr. Splean's office!' Alyssa screamed to me down the hall.

Was this lady not even capable of following her own rules? I guess not.

Just to annoy her I yelled as loud as I could, 'I will.'

She gave me the most judgemental look that she could possibly have gave. Her eyes almost rolled out of her head. So, I guess I had to go there now but what did that lost guy want from me now? Pinned on his door was a huge, framed diploma which I had not seen the other day. Again, he was spinning in his chair I bet he gets paid a huge amount of money but does absolutely nothing. That sounds familiar, just like Mike. But at least what he was doing was legal and as far as I knew did not involve killing or hurting anyone. Except for giving people headaches with his stone hard hands which he hammered one's head with. How many retarded people actually work here? Like till now I had seen so many uncapable nurses, carers, janitors, doctors and well not to forget the voodoo guy.

'Take a seat or do you just want to stand there and stare?'

I should really stop doing that. Well at least I am good at blocking out my environment while I get lost inside my thoughts.

'I got the results of your scans and as you can see here this part of your brain is darker than the others. The structure of your hippocampus and your amygdala is out of the norm. This is a huge indicator that you have suffered a dramatic trauma and have traumatic stress. Have you been extremely hungry lately? Because structural deformation in the amygdala can lead to electrical stimulations in the brain which increase one's appetite.'

He was pointing all over the black and white scan and speaking a hundred miles an hour. Was what he was blabbing true because I was a bit hungrier than I usually was, but I did not have a trauma. And if so, it was from staying in this place. Although what he was saying complied with what had happened to me lately. It probably was just a coincidence. I had eaten far more than normal in the last couple of days. Could all of the bad things have added up to a trauma. Could everything just have become too much? Was I not able to handle it all? Was I weak, had I lost the strength to endure my own life? If I were suffering a trauma, it surely had not just begun but have its roots way back.

'You will need to stay here a while.', he continued, "Then you will get better.".

'How long is a while?', I asked desperately.

'That is always hard to define, but for sure three weeks or even longer. As I already told you, you can leave as soon as you are stable.'

After like one million words from him I was finally allowed to go. I went straight to the park to meet up with Alice. I was dreading seeing her, however I still kinda wanted to. I was slightly early, so I decided to stroll around the garden myself a bit. It was a pretty impressive garden: There were cobblestone paths everywhere, which were bordered with fruit and pine trees. There were also bushes and rose plants. In the middle of the garden there was a big pound where a few ducks swam around. Throughout the park there where multiple benches and also a few picnic tables. When I arrived at the end of the garden, there was a big wall which surrounded the psychiatric hospital so no one could get out. I sat down on the wooden beach which happened to be behind me. I could see the four cement buildings which made up the facilities of the hospital. They were literally four cubes with windows. They all looked the exact same with the exception that the building with the cafeteria had bigger windows, well big glass sliding doors to the outside. This place was nice but still it was a prison. Cause I was not free to leave nor do what I wanted when I wanted. What did I want to do anyway apart from replaying my life? But it was less of a prison for my soul, here my soul was slightly freer than it was at the factory.

I saw Alice from afar. It was impossible to miss her. She really was gorgeous. Her green eyes were so rich in color, and they had this certain twinkle when the sun hit them. Her shoulder long glossy red hair was absolutely phenomenal. But she should really start eating something. Maybe that could be the goal of my stay to help her get out of this prisonlike place. She should experience life in its full glory. She would be an amazing person in real life. In the real world. Well, she was already here. I could see her in a business suit strolling down the roads of New York, being all sassy running some sort of company. Maybe she would work in real estate or maybe she would run a hotel. But certainly, she would be in a leading position using all her attitude to give instructions and commands to her workers.

'How are you, cause I am great, and ready for my story. You can't even imagine my excitement,' she exclaimed.

'Oh gosh, girl. I am not feeling the same,' I responded.

Not at all. I had been dreading this point all night and the whole morning. We walked to a quiet bench which looked over the lake. Well, it was more of a pond. We sat down beside each other hip to hip. She stared into my eyes and looked at me full of hope that I would start telling her my story.

'How much longer are you going to make me wait? Start alright! I cannot wait anymore. I losing patience with you,' she said.

Here we go.

'So let's start at the beginning, after I graduated from high school in Brooklyn. I got into university in New York where I did my bachelor and then my master's in chemistry. I graduated top of my class. After that I got a great job in a pharmacy company there, where I was developing pills to treat cancer. I was working on a drug that would help fight cancer cells. During my time at university, I met Mike.

'Who is Mike?' she asked eagerly.

'Just let me talk, would you. You will understand eventually.'

I didn't know why I was telling her this. It would have been so easy to just stand up and walk away and never need to speak another word to her. She could not make me. But I felt like I was obliged.

'Yess, just continue.', she said.

'So, Mike, he was a genuine guy, well that is what I thought. But anyway, we became really good friends and I introduced him to my uni friends. We started to do things all together and hang out a lot after classes. There was a point where I even thought we were going to end up together. Although that never happened, luckily. Mike was studying engineering. He wanted to become a world-famous engineer and he wanted to become filthy rich. Money was pretty important to him. I don't know when he started turning to illegal stuff for money. But one day he asked me if I could do him a favor. Since I cared a lot about him and had no problem doing something for him, I agreed immediately before even knowing what he wanted me to do. I will never forget this day, the emotions that I felt back then I still cannot sort out in my head. We than drove out of the city into the middle of no-where where there was a small concrete building which was surrounded with trees. He led me inside. At that point I thought he wanted me to help him build something he had designed or that he had this amazing invention he wanted me to test with him. I was hyped. Until he showed me boxes filled with chemicals. I had no idea what he wanted to do with them. He then started to talk about making counterfeit cosmetics and then selling them online and on the black-market as originals. He told me how good the money was and how it wasn't dangerous, how there was no way that we could get caught. I hated the idea. I detested it. He was such a smart guy, why did he need to stuff like this. I saw no way-out Mike had power over me, he played a big role in my life. And we would say love makes you blind and it really does. I knew I was doing wrong, and I knew I could just of said no. But back then no had not accrued as a option to me. I just had closed my eyes and ran against this big black wall without knowing what was awaiting me, hoping that it was just one thing that would be over sooner then we knew it so its memory could become past and start to be forgotten However I was wrong I helped him develop recipes for different mascaras, eyeshadows, and foundations. After I finished, I thought I was done. I thought I would never be involved again. So, I went back to my normal life. But not many days after he came up knocking on my front door. He apologized for what he had done and told me he only did it this one time to have enough money to pay for his last semester. I believed him for some reason. I just thought well everyone makes mistakes, this was his. It was just a small hiccup. I still had this illusion that he was this amazing person.

So, we were friends again, everything was back to normal. I had fully forgiven him for making me get caught up in his illegal affairs, cause you know I had thought good people make mistakes. But Mike was the opposite of good. I was working in the lab for the pharmaceutical company while most of my friends and Mike were in their final year. But we would still meet up like we used to. One day he asked me and my friend if we wanted to join him on a trip to Mexico City. He had whispered in my ear that it was to make up for the things he made me do for the mistakes he had made. He said he wanted to leave his past behind him and the first thing to do so was to make it up to me. He talked about the fact that it was unfair what he did and that he could never make it right. He said that this trip would at least create new memories and let us look in the future. I had believed every word he said. We were all really excited. Apparently, we did not need to pay anything cause he had won the trip. So, we logically all agreed to go. Cause who doesn't want a free trip with friends with no strings attached?

Well, that's at least what we thought. At the airport he gave us each a beach bag. He told us to put in our carry-ons. We were in a rush so he told us he would tell us more about it when we landed. We all did not think much about it and just followed his directions. I should have had thought that something was fishy. Who gives eight people a beach bag to put in their carryon? But at that moment, we were all too busy thinking about the great trip we were going to have. About the amazing food. About the glorious views. About the perfectly white sandy beaches.

Retelling my past was really tiring me out. It sounded so harmless. Felt like I could not even put the emotions I had into words. The things I said just did not totally reflect the reality of what had happened. Mike had been such a different person to me before all of this. I had been in love with him. Maybe that had made me blind. I thought he was one of the best people I had ever met, that I would ever meet. I thought we were going to be friends for life, I had never thought of life without him. Emotions started to flood my body and I did not know what to feel. Did I miss this old Mike? Did a part of me still love him?

'Do I really need to tell you everything?', I asked.

'Every tiny, tiny detail,' she replied.

Gosh, this would take forever! I was afraid that I could not retell it exactly how it was. I was going to tell her my version, but she would never know Mike's. I was in the same situation. I would never know his story. I wondered how different it might be.

'Before security, Mike told us that we should go ahead and then wait for him at the gate cause he had forgotten one of his bags in the car and he wanted to check if our taxi driver was still there. We all thought nothing of it and rushed off. We did not want to complain since he had organized this trip for us, well, and won it. So, we went on through security. Eilin, my best friend went first. Her bag got taken out and she was called to the back. We all thought it was funny cause we thought we knew that nothing was wrong. Like we were expecting there to be a pair of scissors in her vanity bag that she had forgotten. But before we knew it each of us was taken out separately into different rooms. I saw dogs sniffing my bag and security guys going through all our luggage. To cut a long story short – in the beach bags Mike had given all of us, there were drugs and counterfeit cosmetics which we were supposed to smuggle across the border. Mike never came to the security in the airport. I also believe that in Mexico we would not even have had a place to stay cause later I figured out that our flight back was on the same day. After a while, police officers arrived at the airport security check. All our bags were confiscated, and we were taken to the police station where they asked us a ton of questions. They did not believe any of us. They were certain that we knew that we were smuggling. We were sent to prison to wait for their investigation and our trial, that would follow. They were so sure that we were the heads of an outfit that made counterfeit cosmetics and dealt drugs. They had got anonymous tips that we were involved, so that just supported their claims. Wonder where those came from. The number of cosmetics had been minute, but Mike surely had wanted to show them to his dealers as samples. After a couple of days, we had to go to court. Mike was also there since we had all said that he was travelling with us. The police did not believe us though when we tried to explain that he had given us the stuff without us knowing. He had brought his fancy lawyer and somehow managed to pull me out and him of the whole thing. My friends were all sent back to prison. I don't exactly know how many years they got. I think it was a few cause Mikes lovely lawyer had stringed various crimes to them. Plus, I have not had contact with them nor seen them since that day in court.'

My face was starting to feel kinda stiff after all this talking. My jawbone was starting to ace. And my brain was racing one hundred miles per hour after remembering all of this, all of this shit. I would never get over the feeling that I had ruined the lives of people who I was close to.

'Damn, how are you still standing upright after all this, and I have a feeling it's not everything!' Alice exclaimed.

'I don't know, life goes on, but I think I have talked enough for today. Can we please go and eat something? I'm starving.' I tried to get myself out of letting out more emotions.

We started to make our way back to the cafeteria where dinner was being served.

'Now it is your turn to do your part of the deal,' I told Alice.

We both grabbed trays and took fried rice, which looked relatively edible. I was kind of proud when she managed to force a third of the plate down her mouth. After we finished, I went back to my room. I was still alone; I was wondering where they had put Mike cause I still had not seen him again. I was happy that Alice had to help in the kitchen with dishes tonight, so I had some time for myself. I wonder why I did not need to do any chore or job, whatever you want to call it, like her. Well, it was nice not needing to do much in a way. It was detoxing. But I still hoped that I could leave this place soon. I was getting pretty sick of it. Maybe I should change my clothes. They did not smell so pleasant. I remembered Alyssa had told me there were washing machines when she had given me a tour of the psychiatry. Now to find them. Cause maybe I had drifted off while she had showed me around. But what would I do while my clothes were washing? Should I just stand around in my white bra and underwear? Why not? No one was here and probably no one would come wash their clothes at eight-thirty at night, plus it only took a half an hour to run the machine. And I did not care. So, there I was lost in my thoughts standing in underwear beside a washing machine waiting. Leaning to the wall so I could support myself without the crouches. After I had successfully followed the blue arrows painted in the hallways. It was peaceful to listen to the machine turning, just listening to the buttons of the polo shirt hit the metal of the washing machine. I was imagining that I was at the beach and the sound was coming from the water splashing against the rocks. I could see the waves coming to shore hitting my feet and then crawling back into the ocean. I tasted the salt in the air and I could just imagine the sand between my toes. For miles and miles all I could see was blue water that was reflecting the sun. The waves were so peaceful. I had landed in a paradise in my mind. I had probably closed my eyes, I felt warm hands around my waste and suddenly I felt my lips touch someone else's. It felt good so I did not pull away. I just let it happen. I thought it was part of my imagination. The hands started going up and down my back and I became more unsure if I was capable of imagining something that felt so real. The hands met my waist and I felt tingling going through my whole body. I opened my eyes scared to see reality after I had wondered if the feeling would go away. First, I just opened them a little just so some light could come in. After a while I found the courage to open them completely. And what or who I saw shocked me. I did not know what to do. Even though I did not want to close my eyes again they did it on their own. I started to become dizzy and all that appeared before me was black. I started losing the feelings in my leg and lost my balance. I tried catching myself on the ledge of a table but failed. I was no longer leaning on the washing machine that had kept me upright. I fell over without feeling any pain. I had no idea what happened after that. After what felt like an eternity, I was able to open my eyes again. I saw beautiful blue eyes staring straight into mine with a concerned look. I studied the color and the lines that split the eyes into different regions. I then remembered who those blue eyes belonged to. They were taking me back to my little spot in the blue ocean. What had just happened between us. Was it actually real? And why did it feel so good and so wrong at the same time? There was no way I could have feelings for him no way. It must have just been cause he was a good kisser or something like that. If this had happened in those times where I had thought we could end up being something, I would have been thrilled. But those time were definitely over. I was over him. He was a different person to me, a horrible person. I was sickened by myself.

'Are you ok, you fainted and have been unconscious for ten minutes,' he whispered. His eyes were directed towards mine and he had a small smile on his face, but he could not hide his worries.

I just nodded. I had never heard him talk in a so soft, concerned voice. Was this like his identical twin or some kind of joke I did not know about? Was it all just a dream? I was too week to stand up or even move. Without me being able to fight it, he picked me up and carried me to my room. I was fighting myself to not feel comfortable and good. Those were the wrong emotions to be feeling. He gently lay me on my bed and covered me. I fell asleep immediately. Like I was fighting my eyes not to close but I had no chance. They just fell like they both weighed tons.

That night I dreamed. I dreamed about what had happened right in front of the washing machine. I did not know how or what I should feel. I was deeply confused. And my stomach was turning upside-down the whole time, which did not feel good. My life was a huge mess. It seemed like it was always getting more complicated and more messed up. I was like a magnet for dreadful things. And if I tried to do something against it, I messed it up even more. Once again, I was awakened by disinfectant spray plus I realized that I had gotten pretty cold. Probably due to the fact that I was only wearing underwear. I was abandoned. I had been left alone after what had happened. I had made sure to scan every corner of the room with my squinting eyes. When I climbed out of the covers, I was even more freezing. The floor felt ice-cold on my tiny feet, and I could feel the chills going up my entire body. I decided to run down the hall in what I was wearing and hoped my clothes would be in the drier or somewhere in the laundry room. Now I really looked like a lunatic. Like I was someone from here, but I wasn't, was I?

On my way down the hall, I got a few looks. But I just kept running. I was determined to get my clothes. Well, if you can call what I was trying do with crutches running. There was no time to look back. I took a turn to the left and almost slipped in the corner. Thank God I had a second pair of crutches in my room cause the others were also probably still in the laundry room. After nearly falling over, I ran into the laundry room and immediately spotted my clothes on top of one of the machines. I put them on and went straight back to my room to sort my thoughts a bit, plus to warm up under my cover. I had gotten quite sweaty and hottish after my sprint, but the sweat had made me cold as soon as I had calmed down. When I finally was all cozy in my bed, I realized that I had not looked for my crutches in the laundry room. Well, I guess that would be a chore for later.

So, wait a minute, I was standing almost naked in a laundry room and made out with a criminal who ruined quite a few things in my life. That was so wrong. Oh, wait and all of this happened inside of a psychiatric institution. Oh and a few days back he almost killed me. What kind of personality does Mike have? Was he always softer to me than to the others because he felt something for me? Had he given me better housing than the others cause of that? But why would he get me into illegal stuff if he had feelings for me? Would he not then want the best for me. Why would he harm me if deep down he loved something about me? Why had he given me a near death experience if what I was thinking was the truth? What was wrong with him? This was too much to take in. What was I supposed to do? What? If I were religious, I would probably have prayed by now. But I am not. What was I going to do? I got sooo overwhelmed that I started to walk back and forth in my room like a tiger locked up in a cage. In the end I found myself sitting on the floor staring at the ceiling – my brain full and totally empty at the same time.

The overload of emotions and thoughts had probably led to me falling asleep. Cause I woke up lying on the floor. My back was aching, and I had cramps everywhere. How was I able to sleep on this stone-hard, ice-cold floor? I managed to get up after a few struggles and fails. I climbed back on my bed and stared at the wall. I still could not understand what had happened. Like what? Everything just did not make sense. I started to feel my stomach grumbling. Well, that was no surprise. I had skipped breakfast and had no idea what time it was already. It took a huge effort for me to get to the canteen. Why did I have to lose one leg? Things would be a lot easier with two. Also, my tailbone was aching, probably from the unhealthy position I had slept in. I made it to the canteen and for the first time I read the electronic menu. I made my way in the line where there were all kinds of patients waiting for their food. Alice was definitely not the only girl here that suffered from anorexia, or some kind of eating disorder. In front of me there were three girls lined up who all looked like piles of bones with a bit of skin. It must be so hard for them. I wonder which was worse – being underweight like these girls or being morbidly obese like some of the other patients I had seen here? Well maybe I would prefer their problems over mine. I grabbed the mac and cheese and some carrots and went to the table by the window. Like always. Once again I started devouring my food. When I finished stuffing my face I just sat for a while and stared outside. I started to notice the huge resemblance between this canteen and the canteen that I had gone to in high school. The same plastic tables and benches. Similar size. The food tasted identical. They probably bought their ingredients from the same company or used some unified menu. The atmosphere although was different. There weren't kids screaming and babbling the whole time. But there was more like a tense vibe in the air. And a quietness which sometimes was interrupted by someone talking to themselves or someone having a tantrum or something like that. This was definitely a weird place with peculiar people. Was I like the other patients here? Was I that off the rails, out of my box? I don't know. Did I care? Also no, and no one would really judge me here. Their brains were, let's say, a bit out of the norm, maybe not even functioning. Well, what was with my brain then, did it belong to another universe? But at least I could enjoy the view, the garden was truly remarkable. I hope everyone appreciated it like I did. Like just take a look out of the window. The plants are incredible, and the colours are just stunning. How the sun hits the pound and all the greens from the trees. And then all the bushes that are blooming and all the flowers in full bloom. Just imagine if you were colour-blind then what would trees look like what would anything look like? That was one more thing I did not understand. Well, I wanted to know and understand but on the other hand I did not care. I was just watching the birds drinking from a small bird fountain which was beside one of the benches that were situated around the pound. I was so mesmerizing to watch them. They would sit on branches on the trees than fly down to the fountain. Jump in or just stick their head down to sip water. It was kinda cute.

'Hey, are you going to join me for a walk, or better said a story telling session.' I was startled.

Alice was standing beside me and had put her hand on my shoulder. I turned to her. This girl was very determined to figure out my whole life story. Very nosy. But you know what, as long as she would eat something, I would be willing to tell her my story. I think. So, I got up and followed her outside. When we passed through the glass sliding doors. I realized I had not put my tray away. I thought about going back to do so but then I figured it would be no big deal and just forgot about it. So much for following the system.

'So how much longer is your silence going to last?' Alice said.

Gosh, she was impatient! Soo impatient.

'First you're going convince me that you actually ate something for lunch today.'

'Of course, I had an entire bowl of pasta. Which is a lot for me. Proud?' she answered with a grin right across here cheeks.

'Well proud you did your part of deal. I am kidding of course. I am so happy for you. I think you will be better in no time if you continue like this.'

'I will be better when you continue telling your story.'

We continued walking to the same beach where we had sat last time. I did not want to talk. I just wanted to stand up and run. I wanted to be alone. I wanted to disappear to someplace where no one knew me and I would not know myself.

'So where was I?' I asked against my will.

I had totally forgotten where we had left off. Too much had happened in the meantime. 'You were telling me about how your friends who were sent to prison, and you got off free.'

'Oh ya, I remember. So, after court I went straight to my apartment so I would not need to face Mike. I didn't even want to look at him. Just the sound of his name would me make me want to tear up or punch something. I opened the door to my apartment and flopped down on my stomach on my bed and started to cry. I was so disappointed in myself. I had managed to pull my friends into something which led them to prison. Which would most likely ruin their lives. I was soo depressed, to be honest. I can't even explain to you how bad I felt. I did not know how to deal with the situation. On the one hand I was happy that I was not in prison but on the other it was not fair at all. I just felt horrible. I ended up calling in sick for work for an entire week. I cried all day and night in bed. My blankets and pillows were drenched, it was soo revolting. But I had no energy to get up and fix it. I thought my life was over. After seven horrendous days I finally managed to get up and go to work. The following months I lived like a ghost. I went to work. Never really talked to anyone. Went home, ate and slept. My social life totally died. I never went out. I just lived in my own despair. Many times, I thought of visiting my friends. But I was too afraid of their reactions. I was afraid of the reality. If I look back now though I regret not going to see them. They were really good friends. Most likely they would have believed me and forgiven me. I live with so much regret now for not going to see them. Like I could at least have gone to say sorry.'

I started to burst out in tears. I had felt them coming. My eyes burned, and the trees started to become blurry in front of me. I felt the drops of water run down my cheeks. I started to taste the salt from the tears on my lips. My face was burning. I had leaned my head on Alice's shoulder and had made her entire polo shirt wet. I felt her arm over me. She was holding me safe and comforting me. It was a long time since I had been able to live in the present and appreciate someone so deeply like I did at that moment.

'Darling, its ok, don't worry I am here for you. Whatever you need,' Alice said softly.

Alice had a good heart. She understood me a bit. I think. I don't know how long she held me in her arms but to me the concept of time had been lost.

'Mia are you a bit better cause we should probably go inside, it's getting dark,' she said in a hushed tone.

I looked up, tried to see something through all my tears. The surroundings were still blurry. But was definitely darker. I could see the silhouettes of the buildings. What time was it? Had we just sat outside the hole afternoon? I hoped Alyssa had not been looking for me. I did not want to get on her bad side, cause I was pretty sure she had an influence on when I could leave. Soon, I hoped.

'Mia? Alice whispered, let's go inside.'

As we entered the building my sight finally started to clear up. I did not deserve to be treated so well. Alice accompanied me all the way to my room, which I still had to myself. Had they not told me when I arrived that there was limited space? Well, if the space was so limited why was I still alone? I should not jinx it. I wanted to keep the room to myself. I just lay in bed. Alice covered me. I felt so safe. I felt warm. I could feel the warmth in my entire body. It felt good. The feeling was totally different compared to when Mark had covered me yesterday. It was more real more genuine, more wanted. After a long time, I could fall asleep without getting lost in my thoughts. I did not even dream. My head was empty. It felt such a relief. I did not feel scared to wake up the next morning.

GIVE ME A BREAK

Disinfectant, gosh. Back to reality. My peace of mind had not lasted for very long. Before I knew it, I was thinking about three things at the same time. And then thinking of why I was thinking and why I was thinking about what I was thinking about why I was thinking that. Actually, what was wrong with me? I am pretty sure that's not normal. Could my thoughts just take a break? Well, they had yesterday. Well, another break. Please. I don't want to think about Mike. Mike. Mike. I was trying to hold my head so my thoughts would not explode completely, for once I was thankful that Alyssa entered. I was relieved that I had been staring through the small window on the door cause that had given me enough time to stop holding my head awkwardly and sit up in my bed. Alyssa gave me her usual speech and I answered with my usual answer, ok. This time she added somewhat rudely, 'You have an appointment with Dr.Splean at eleven. I advise you to take a shower.'

Did it smell so bad in here? Well, I smelt my own sweat. That was maybe not the best sign. I think my feet also reeked a bit from the athlete's-foot I had probably gotten from not changing my socks. And from always wearing moist socks. Ok, she was right, I did smell. Which was disgusting. But if I had deodorant, it would make it a tiny bit better. I stood up and made my way to the showers. But I would not tell her that she was right. I noticed that my shirt was still moist from all my tears yesterday. There were also some stains from sweat and tears and other stuff all over it. How did that happen exactly? The warm water started to fall down my shoulders and for a moment I could empty my mind again until I realized I was not thinking much. I felt each drop of lukewarm water hit my shoulders and roll down my body till it hit the floor of the shower. I watched the water with excitement. My thoughts started to spiral again. I was getting more and more sure that this was not healthy. My head started to feel heavy again and almost dizzy. Fainty. Turney. I heard thumping steps approaching my room. Did people need to walk like they were obese? No offence to overweight people. Well just a little bit. I should stop offending people. It's a bad habit. Well at least I offended and judged most people inside of my head and did not tell them directly to their face did not know if that was any better though was that better though. A nurse I had never seen before opened the door.

'Hello Mia, I will be taking you to Dr. Splean today. My name is Cassandra.'

She was obese. Was it just me or did obese people always talk in a different tone and have a certain smell? Like maybe a bit of fast food. I don't know. This nurse was definitely not pretty. She smiled at me and all I saw is a set of yellowish teeth. Repulsive. Brush your teeth lady. Toothpaste costs like 1 dollar not even. Today Dr. Splean was actually writing something. Maybe occasionally he actually did the work he was being paid for. Or he just did enough not to be fired. Both could be possibilities.

'Good morning, Mia. How are you feeling today?', he said in his most friendly voice.

Why did everyone need to know how I was doing, I did not even know myself. Is it such an important aspect? Well maybe it is but whatever.

'Ok.'

I entered his office while Cassandra, the fat nurse, closed the door after me. Not very gently. Again, I heard her thumping away. Was her goal to break the floor?

'Please lie down Mia,' he ordered.

I obeyed his instructions and sat down on the examination table which was covered with one of those paper sheets. When I sat my ass on it you could hear the paper crinkle up. Honestly, the paper also felt pretty uncomfortable though my sweatpants. I could feel the wrinkles.

'Mia, I would like you to tell me how your therapy sessions are going with Dr. Clark.'

Who, what? Ohh the yoga slash hippie dude. I had had like four sessions with him. Every time it was the same thing. He would ask questions. And I would try to invent answers that made some sort of sense. I was basically trying to make up a story that would look like I was 'getting better' or whatever. I was not quite sure if it was working. But they would never know that I was making up most of what I said. They would need to trust that I was telling the truth. I wasn't but they would not know. They never needed to know. I anyway think I needed to heal on my own. If I need to heal. I am mental anyway. I can't just stop my thoughts, forget about the things that have happened to me. Just not gonna work girl. But to be honest some of my lies were based on real things. You know like the movies, based on a real-life story. Sometimes I was not even sure what was real and what wasn't anymore. There was no clear line. So, if I didn't know if I was lying, was I lying? Gosh. I was mental.

'Good, I think it's really helping me. I feel a lot less anxious. And I don't get angry as quickly as I did before. I am starting to actually appreciate it and understand why I am here,' I answered.

'I am glad to hear, he said, so about your appointment with me today. I would like to try and see if you can recall any memories from that horrible night. It's not just for you but the police are still running investigations and they think if you saw anything you could be very useful to them.'

What was it? I was many things. I was seeing Dr. Splean right now, I saw a wall right now, I saw my hand. I saw loads. I was not blind or at least in theory. Oh, so now I was a useful object. Maybe that is why they are keeping me here, cause they need me to solve the case. But I was not going to help them cause they would never believe me. They would only believe what they wanted to believe. I did not remember everything, but the majority of that night had come back to me. Well of course to the point where a knife was stabbed in my back. But what I found odd was that there was no scar or anything like that on my back. Wait a minute, when I woke up here, there was not even an open spot in my skin. Well, I had not looked at it very carefully but ... How? What now? I was even more confused. I felt Mike put a knife in my back I was soo sure. I remember the thoughts like it was yesterday. This needed to be cleared up. I hated when things did not make sense in my head. Well, a lot of things didn't. But this had to be clear in my head, what had happened. What was reality what had I imagined and made up. How could I have forgotten that I had almost died? How could I have managed to not check my wound even if it was just out of curiosity? I had died a million times in my dreams – in my good dreams not in my nightmares.

'I still don't remember what happened. All I know is that I was on my way to take out my trash and then I have no more memory of what happened.'

'Where were you taking the trash out from?' he asked.

I could just barely stop myself from saying my apartment. That would not have ended well. I had to be careful with my lies. Very careful. I couldn't be exposed. Then they would never let me out of there. They wouldn't even understand the difference between reality and lies. They don't even know that now. They think they understand, they think that they can see in my head but in fact they haven't got a clue. Think fast Mia. The longer you wait the less real your answer will sound. Say something. You're smart. Figure it out. Quick, isn't there a hostel right beside the bakery that is across from the police station. Got it.

'I was staying in a friend's hostel room cause she had left New York three days earlier, she had left all a couple of things behind. She had asked me to just throw some things away so I would not need to carry them around with me until we would meet again. So, I had collected them and went out to put them in one of the garages. The one beside the hostel was overflowing with garbage, so I went to look for the next nearest one.'

That was a good lie. I think. I will just give myself credit that I was a good liar. Was that a good thing?

'Why were you staying in a hostel?' he asked.

This is not going to end well. I would have to remind myself to get my story straight this evening. Study it. Repeat it. Remember it. Make it reality.

'I had been backpacking through the US for the past two and a half years.'

That made sense, that's when I got out of prison. So, if they would ask about my felony. I would say I needed a break from work and all this, so I had decided to use up saved money to do a trip through the US. My cover story was starting to make sense. It just had to be believable and not traceable. Dr. Splean just nodded and wrote more notes on his clipboard. He was one of those people who wrote very loudly. He was almost breaking his pen. If there was more paper underneath one could probably read everything he wrote.

'Can you really not recall anything from the incident, a sound, a face, even just a smell?' What could I say that made sense?

'I remember Mike's face, but other than that I just recall blood passing over my face and then the picture is just black. If that makes any sense.'

Now, shit I should have not said his name. If this Splean asks me about Mike everything will break, how would I know his name if I had not known him before. Oh no. Mia watch out.

'It does, it all has a reason, it is due to a defence mechanism which is activated in situations like these. I will give you this medication, it's supposed to enhance the brain's function. Sometimes it helps one recall things and get memories back.'

He was trying to sound smart; I think. Like did he even know the name of the pill? Where did this guy get his degree? Or ya, it might be fake. That was not the first time that that crossed my mind. He explained that I needed to take the pill in the morning at eight before breakfast and right after dinner in the evening. He also asked me another million questions before I was allowed to leave with my container of pills. At least he had not asked anything about Mike. I swayed to my room with the pills hitting the outside of the container with every step I made. I did not intend to take those pills. My brain was already working, it did not need to be enhanced. Relieved I sat down on my bed. But before I could relax, I remembered. I stripped my shirt off and stumbled over to the mirror which hung above the sink. As I got closer ma heart started racing faster. I was so scared of what I was going to see. Nothing. There was nothing to be seen on my back. Wait. No. No there was just a small red spot. What? It just looked like a small bite from some sort of insect or something. Just a bit bigger and a bit redder. It was a different red. I could not describe it to myself. I was in shock. I tried different distances from the mirror, but it did not change anything. I needed to find Mike. I needed to know what had happened. Would he tell me the truth? Well, it was worth a try. I could not let this stand like this. I was determined to find him so I put my shirt back on and walked as fast as I could with my crutches. I walked through all the hallways I was allowed to walk through and some I was not supposed to. I checked the cafeteria, the garden. I even tried to sneak in the men's bathroom. That though was a let-down cause a nurse caught me and said, 'Dear you must have mixed up the bathrooms', and directed me to the women's bathroom. Gosh, I did not need to go pee. I needed to know what happened. He was nowhere to be found. Where was he hiding, maybe he was actually hiding from me. Was he embarrassed? Maybe he just had been so desperate, it did not even matter that it was me. But what I still could not figure out is how I let it happen. I could have stopped him, but I had not. I had wanted more. In that moment it was as if he was a totally different person. Maybe it was not Mike. No, it was Mike. Surely. I lost the hope of finding him and went back to my room to rest my leg. I lay down and again I found myself staring at the wall. What did I see in those drawings? I kept finding myself looking at them. Gosh Mia. Do I need to question everything? And can you stop always talking to yourself about yourself. Please. Stop. I turned my head to the other side because my neck had started to ache. And there I saw Alice peering through the bars. As soon as she met my eyes she entered. She must have thought I was sleeping or something like that. She had remembered me of like a horror movie scene who just stand in front of the door staring that is just creepy.

'I just wanted to make sure you were awake; don't worry I am not a creep. Wanna go for a walk, or you want to continue your story here?'

What else should I have expected? I should have not turned around. Could I not be left alone?

'Let's go,' I said with a little too much fake excitement.

'I was hoping for that answer. I was not sure if it was appropriate to ask because of yesterday, but I could not wait to figure out how it continues.'

We went out through the cafeteria window or door or whatever architects would call it. We found ourselves sitting on the same bench as the previous days. For a moment I just took in the calming feeling the garden gave me. I wondered should I tell her about what had happened between me and Mike, but then after a few turns in my head I thought it would be better if I didn't, because I did not even understand it myself. Yes, that was the right decision.

'I will try not to be too emotional today.'

'Don't worry. I will be here for you. You don't need to play the strong girl for me. I know you're strong, stronger than almost any other person I've met. Probably the strongest. And I am not just saying this to make you feel better. I mean it.'

Here we go into my deep pool of emotions. This was really the first time I was retelling the story to anybody than myself.

'So, I was basically living but not really. And definitely not enjoying life. I thought about suicide, but I could not bring myself to do it. The only thing that kept me going was the medications for cancer treatments I was working on. I really thought I would help a lot of people with these pills I was developing. It was the one goal I still had. Especially cause most of my friends had been so proud of this, and had loved this about me. But, it was never reached. Because before I knew it my life was turned upside down again. I had just gotten home from work and emptied my mailbox. There was the usual, bills, magazines, advertisements

But I could not believe my eyes when I opened a letter ordering me to come court again. My case had been reopened. What was that supposed to mean? I had been so confused in that moment. I did not understand. Somehow they had found new evidence.'

'So, wait that means they thought you were guilty?' she asked.

'Indeed. Later, I figured out that Mike had tipped me off. But till today I don't understand why the first time I got out with nothing and then he snitched on me and gets me into prison.' This was the third thing I needed to ask Mike. I needed my past clear as well as the present basically. It just did not make sense why save me from prison if you are going to sent me to prison later.

'So, I went to court mortified, scared, anxious. And I was right to be. I spent 3 years in prison. It was a horrible experience. Prisons are not nice places. And if I had at least been in the same prison as my 'friends', well I don't know if that would have been better but maybe then I could have collected enough courage to at least apologize. The women's prison that I was in was filled with druggies. I saw them dealing and taking it all day long. And I don't think the guards gave a ff. The place was so poorly kept, and it reeked everywhere. And if you would shower without shoes or something on your feet you were guaranteed some sort of foot fungi or warts or something. It just was horrible. There is nothing else to add to it. The only thing is I thought I deserved it. I think I did but on the other hand after I left prison that punishment should have been over. The only reason I had felt guilty was because I had pulled my friends into it. There was no other reason.'

I was about to tell her about the day that I had gotten out of prison. But I saw danger approaching. Alyssa. She could not know anything about it. I gave Alice a look that we needed to change the subject. Fast. After a few glances she caught on and started talking about the chirping birds. She was definitely not dumb.

'Mia, do you agree that the blue jay just have amazing voices?'

Alyssa walked past us with an lady in a wheelchair in about her 50es. She was obese. She must be addicted to food. I did not like that I always judged overweight people, but I just could not stop myself. I knew that a few people could not be blamed for being there size but most of them were just eating themselves to death. I know it was addiction bla bla and they could not stop themselves. But still how could someone not stop eating before they were like dying. I just did not understand but again I never had been in that situation. I loved judging but I hated myself for it. Mia snap back to the moment!

'You are really afraid of people knowing your story, you know it might be good if they know, in my opinion. But I'll leave it up to you.'

She understood a lot of things but in this case, she did not know what she was dealing with. Even I wasn't aware that it was something I never wanted anyone to know. Well, now Alice would know it, but the story should not spread further. I was too afraid of the negative affects it could have on me or others. I already tried to expose Mike and that did not go at all well. I just want him to go to prison. But did I still want that? My brain was a mess. I needed to set a few things straight up there; I needed to find Mike soon. Very soon.

I think Allyssa had brought the obese lady back in, but she just had interrupted our silence. 'Could both of you go in to have dinner, please?'

We followed her instructions and went to have dinner. We ate in silence. I think Alice was also lost in her mind or she was just tired. But I made sure she was eating, and she was. It gave me such euphoria seeing her finish almost her entire plate. It felt that through my dark stories I had achieved something. Something positive for once. It felt soo good. I could feel warmth and satisfaction spread through my body. I left dinner happy until I remembered my mess in my head and that I needed to figure out, well also I wanted to find Mike. So, I was staggering through the hallways of the institution, feeling pretty hopeless. Well, I was hoping to see Mike somewhere. I thought maybe I would just bump into him by coincidence. I was trying to imagine what he would say. If he would explain himself. Would he? I was just more confused the more I thought of that night. I had tried to replay the situation in my head, but I was not sure about a few things and some of the details just seemed to have disappeared. After what felt like forever I gave up. My shoulders were aching, and I couldn't think anymore. I just couldn't. I was way too tired to continue. And I was not going to push myself. Not for Mike. Well, why did I want to know so badly? Why was I not feeling so much hate as I used to when I thought of him? Was I brainwashed? Hypnotized? What had happened. I still hated him. He had ruined my life. I could remember the day he came to get me out of prison like it was yesterday. It was a normal Wednesday. I ate dry bread, an apple and a glass of milk for breakfast, then I had worked my hours in the canteen preparing lunch. I ate lunch. I think we had like some sort of potato mixed with beans and something else brown. Not very tempting to be honest. The afternoon I had spent my free time outside staring at the sky just waiting for another boring day to end and for a new one to begin. Around four, a guard had called me from my cell that I had shared with eight other women. He said I had a visitor. I was surprised because visitors usually only came on Saturday and had never had a visitor. When I had gone off to university, I had literally had no more contact to my family. I could not stand them. I just isolated myself from them. I did not even know if they really knew what had happened to me. Well, so I had followed the guard to the visitors' room on the north side of the prison.

I recognised him from far away back then like I still would today. I could see his blue eyes shimmering: Just as if you were looking at the water from a bungalow in the Maldives. But as soon as I had snapped out of my fantasies I was back in reality. Looking at the man who had turned my life upside down. Who had taken so much. And back then I had not understood why he could not just leave me alone, let me be in prison, live a boring, lonely life, but no, he had other plans for me.

At that moment I just wanted to turn and run in the opposite direction. I finally made it back to my room which I still had for myself. Going down this memory lane had not gone well. I thought I could think about something else in my room but I did not feel at home here, I did not feel safe. I saw the cigarette drawing on the wall and the desire for a smoke flashed through my mind. I had never smoked. But maybe it would have calmed me. But then my brain was racing about the things it would do to my lungs, my brain, my health. I did not understand my own thinking. But before I could debate in my head even more with myself about how smoking would feel like I was back years ago in the visitors' room standing face to face with the man who was to blame for me being here. The officer had mumbled something, but I had not quite been able to make out what he had said. But if I look back, he must have said something about the time I had and some forms and some mistake. I don't know. But that guard had left the room while an officer appeared. He gestured me and Mike to follow him. Everything happened in silence. Except the orders I had been given by the officer. He stripped-searched me the same way they had done when I was incarcerated. Mike had watched with pleasure. Back then I thought he was enjoying it because I was embarrassed and just felt exposed. But now I was thinking he might have watched with greed in his eyes for other reasons. Why had he even been there like I don't know but had he told the officers that I was his girlfriend or sister or mother? I don't know. I still did not know why exactly I had gotten out. Afterwards, I had whimpered about being touched everywhere. Everywhere. I was given a bucket with the clothes I had worn the day I had arrived in prison. I was ordered to change and then I had been told to sign this and that with Mike's eyes never losing sight of me. He had stared at me until I had completed everything. He took me to his car, and we drove off. In silence, I don't know why I could not bring myself to say something, ask, at least insult. I just couldn't, and it hadn't seemed to bother him. We drove and drove, after a while I had forgotten that I was in a car with Mike and had fallen asleep. I slept longer and better than in I had long time. Prison had been hard on me. I had woken up in an office. The office that I would go to every morning from that day on. I just wish I could forget all of this and start over. I could not handle these memories, nor could I accept my present situation in the psychiatry.

UNCHERISHED MEMORIES

It seemed like time was standing still in the clinic. Every day had become the same. Visits at Doctor Splean's office. Walks with Alice. Although we had started talking about other things than my past, it was still the main topic. But as the days passed our walks became shorter or as Alice got weaker and weaker.

One day I had been waiting for her, but she never arrived. Two days later I found out by hounding Alyssa with questions that she was in intense care. I imagined her attached to machines being force fed. That poor girl. She had to make it. I could not lose the one friend I had made in a long time. A week had passed since I had last seen Alice and I was starting to get worried. My days became even more grey. My thoughts even darker. This was the opposite of therapy. And still, I could not find Mike. I had spent so many hours wandering through the institution trying to find him, to the extent that the carers and nurses locked my door at ten o'clock because they thought I was sleepwalking. I was walking in the night but consciously which I do not consider sleepwalking. And I was getting more impatient. I wanted to set things straight with Mike. And I wanted to see Alice. My goal was not anymore to get out of this place. But to figure out my past, meet Alice and help her get out and then get out myself and start over. But I was far from my goals. It was 10.32. I was locked in my room alone. Lonely. Lost in my thoughts. Remembering all the years I had worked for Mike, the days I had spent in the bunker, my escape, my incarceration. I had replayed my past so many times to myself, trying to figure out the missing information. But I was missing the reason why. The why from Mike, why he had done this to me. I was missing his character, I had known him for so long but to me he did not have a personality anymore but multiple pieces of personalities. I did not get it. It was like I had encountered various people, but he was one single person. The day I had woken up in his office after he had picked me up from prison the previous day, he had smiled at me as if I was his best friend, as if he had been the nicest person to me. I did not get it. But those seconds of friendliness had passed quickly. He had called some guy Black, tall. Scary. Later I had figured out it was Fergus. And if I had known him, I would have not been so terrified as I was in that moment. I had not known better. He had grabbed me by my arm and dragged me to the bunker where I had seen hundreds of people stacked on top of each other in bunks, it was worse than prison down there. It had been dark; it had smelled like fungus and there had been dirt everywhere. He had showed me my bed and had brushed my face and had said, 'You'll be fine girl, you're strong. You belong here.'

He had left. I did not know where I should go or what I should do. I did not even know where I was. I just had started shouting and stomping, having a tantrum like a three-year-old girl. I think the others had gotten fed up with me and had started yelling at me to shut the f up. I had sat down on the yellow, green-stained mattress and tried to stay conscious despite the smell. I had already thrown up when I had first sniffed the putrid air. But eventually I was woken up by Mikes insults. He commanded me around. He showed me the grounds of the factory. The Bunker, the different production stages in the factory. I felt like a horse in a ring being followed by a whip, scared of the consequences. I found out he was making counterfeit makeup here. Oh, and drugs, lots of chemical drugs. And I found out my job. I had rebelled, it was the first time since I was there that I had said something to him. I had screamed, yelled, told him he was hurting people. Poisoning people. I had started running, running as far as I could. I still had 2 legs back then I tried to escape. That was one of the last times my brain had been empty. The last time I taught I was doing the right thing. The counterfeiting and working in the factory had not yet become reality, I had not realized yet where I stood. I had gotten all the way to

New York. I had lived on the streets for three weeks till I realized I could not work anywhere. I was initially scared no one would employ me because of my past, my criminal record, but I soon realized I had no documents. It was like I had been erased by society. That's how I found myself walking back to the factory. My body was starved, the rings under my eyes pitch black. I had been raped, I had been awake for days. I felt awful. I did not feel worthy of anything anymore. All my self-respect had been left on the streets. I don't know why I had chosen to go back to Mike. I could have tried to get documents or something. But I had lost hope. Mike was going to come for me eventually. But I think he had known that I would be back sooner or later and that's why he had not made any efforts to catch me. I felt like it was my destiny.

I arrived and Mike came to get me, and I was thrown into the bunker. He had called one of his guys, he was a boss of one part of the factory he had looked me in the eyes with some sort of pity. Mike yelled at him in a language I did not speak. I had felt pain rushing through my body. He just had shot my leg multiple times. Blood started gushing all over and I fell to the ground. Mike had turned his back to me and was now walking away without even glimpsing at what had happened. I saw blood everywhere; the pain was unbearable. I heard a faint voice say, 'You'll never run away like this again.' A few of the factory workers who had either seen or heard the shots had dropped everything they were doing and had come running. They had wanted to help. But I had not appreciated it and had been screaming at them not to touch me. I could feel my heartbeat everywhere in my body. And then unexpectedly the pain started to stop, I could not feel anything anymore. I started to get dizzy, and I could still see but no longer hear. A big black figure had picked me up and had been carrying me. Someone had put wet clothes with some sort of chemical over my mouth which made me pass out. By the time I woke up my leg was gone. Fergus was sitting on the side of my bed and some middle-aged black woman was disinfecting my wound. Fergus explained to me that his wife had been a nurse in her earlier life and that he had served in the army and that they had to amputate my leg because they couldn't remove the bullets and they were afraid of an infection and since they could not take me to a hospital it would be the safest option and only option. I had cried and cried. Three days I just lay in the bunker. I had got use to the smell and every night Fergus and his wife would come. They would bring me food, tend to my wound, try and encourage me. I did not understand the compassion they had. They seemed happy even though they were looked like their ancestors – forced to work, forced to breathe in chemicals, forced to be here. Forced to live.

I wondered how. They just did everything so effortlessly as if it was like they did not even mind. Even though I had not thanked them even once I appreciated them from the bottom of my heart. No one had been so nice to me in a long time. On the second day I had asked Fergus about how he had ended here, and he had told me that I would have to be patient and then one day I would understand. On the third day I had gotten up with the others. I could no longer feel self-pity. I had to accept the situation the way it was. I remembered every detail of what I had been told to do. So, I got up and did it like I had been doing it for years. I had stumbled up to the office with some crutches one younger girl, Lilian, had found for me. The people here were empathetic, sad and depressed but they cared for one another. I had admired their way of dealing with situations. I went to the office down the hall to get a sample of the real makeup that I was supposed to create a counterfeit recipe for. I had gone to the lab that I had been shown the other day. And had started trying, experimenting, calculating. It was not the first time I had done this. But it had felt more real now. There was no going back. At least my passion for chemistry was somewhat useful. And in the beginning, I had tried to use stuff that was less toxic but over time I had no other choice and I started not to care anymore. It was like when I was working at the pharmaceutical company after my friends were sent to prison. Day in day out was the same. Life did not matter. A week had passed. I had mixed up two new recipes. Mike came down to the bunker one evening calling me to pack up. I was so afraid as I followed him through the woods that surrounded the factory. But on the other hand, I was enjoying being away from the horrible smells that lurked in the factory and in the bunker. I was able to smell the woods. The earth, the freshness. So, I had tried to enjoy it. And I did not fear death, I lived for nothing anyway. As we approached a small house, he said it was mine to stay in. I was so surprised and happy. This little thing was huge for me. Well, it was more than just a little thing. I could not stand staying in the bunker. And I had voiced that to Mike several times when I had seen him around the factory. It was more to get rid of my anger. I had never thought I would achieve anything with it. Some of the others had warned me of talking to Mike that way and had reminded me of what had happened to my leg. But I had not cared. And after I had gotten the house, I had been even happier. I was bad at listening to others. My mind was strong and would do whatever it thought was right. I settled in. Everything was still a bit dusty and run down, but it did not smell like fungus and mould which was an enormous improvement and I had space. My own space. Mike's vibe was weird that evening and it appeared as if he wasn't going to leave but eventually, he did.

I had not questioned it back then but now I was sceptical. I heard a carer unlock my door in the psychiatry and I was torn out of my memories. He asked the usual question that I answered as usual. I was fed up, I wanted to leave. Alyssa came in moments later. And I started begging. All this place was doing to me was giving me room to think about my past, and all I wanted to do at most was avoid every thought that had to do anything with it.

'Please let me see Alice, it will make me feel so much better, please,' I pleaded.

After me begging to her in all the ways I knew how to beg, she agreed.

'OK, I will let you see her, but you can't tell anyone that I am doing this for you. I don't want to lose my job for something like this.'

I thought she was going to say for someone like you. I followed her to a part the psychiatric institution I had never been before. Maybe I would see Mike. Mia snap out of it! You are here for Alice. She is more important than Mike. Was she? I really need to stop thinking of him. Dreaming of him. It was not healthy. I saw Alice lying on a bed attached to multiple tubes. There were tubes going into her arm with some clear liquid. There were tubes up her nose. There was a machine attached to her that read the heart rate, I think. I started to feel sick. I felt my stomach flip upside down. I started to get cold and shiver. She looked so bad. She looked like she was dead, her face was so pale. Her body as bony as I had ever seen. Her hair as brittle as it could be. It seemed as if you would touch her, she would break. So fragile. Alyssa whispered to me that I should follow her into the room. I sat down on the side of Alice's bed and took her hand. I felt her slow heartbeat on her wrist.

'Alice, I need you, and I need you so that I can finish my story. You have helped me, now it is my turn. You can't leave the world girl. You got so much potential so many more lovely things in front of you.'

I was disappointed when she did not answer but what could I expect? But when I looked at her face, I saw a small smile, a smirk. It filled my heart with warmth. I squeezed her hand. I had forgotten about the fragile thoughts I had had before. I felt her almost wasted muscles react back but before I could enjoy the moment fully Alyssa had ushered me out of the room because another nurse was coming. We dashed away. Tears started to fall. If they were of fear, sadness or joy no one would ever know. I was soo thankful that I was able to see Alice, but I was sure Alyssa thought I was taking it for granted. But I was not. Not at all. Alice was so beautiful, so smart, gifted, she deserved life, unlike me. I wanted her to get better. So badly. Alyssa led me back to my room and went without a word. That whole day the only thing going round in my mind was the picture of Alice attached to all the tubes. Only half alive. I felt guilty for some reason. I started blaming myself. Started questioning the point of life again, of my existence. I had wanted to help her heal but I had failed. She was in a worse condition than she was when I had arrived. Had I done that to her? Had my stories made her more stressed? Had the stress made her use up more calories? Had this led to the state that she was in? She had to get better, there was no other way. I could not watch this happen. She deserved more. More than me. Life was not fair. What was the point if the things we were always working for were just taken away from us? Why was life so hard? Did it have to be this way? My emotions started spiralling off and that is how I found myself lying under the bed in my room glaring at the wooden bars that held the mattress. I did not even know how I ended up lying under the bed. But that is where I was. And I was not moving anywhere. I just wanted to be absorbed by the floor. Into the dark. Into the nothing. I could not stand this world anymore. It was too much to handle, too much for me. I was not made of strong enough material. I was weaker than I had thought. I just can't anymore. I can't. The tears were running down my face. My head was hurting from my thoughts. I felt pain in my stomach and chest. I felt as if my body wanted to throw up all over the place. I was already imagining how the vomit would rise, hit the wooden things and then fall and hit my face.

'Mia, you will need to go to Dr. Splean's office at three o'clock. Mia, Hello?'

That lady scarred the shit out of me. I tried to sit up and hit my head on the wooden planks which held the mattress. And fell back down on to the ground. Now I could feel my heartbeat rising to my head and pounding in a fast rhythm. I saw Alyssa peering under the bed with an expression of total confusion on her face. I felt the embarrassment rush through my blood.

'Mia what on earth are you doing under the bed?' she asked.

I told her that I had probably fallen asleep and rolled out of bed somehow. Was that somewhat believable? Whatever. I did not even know myself how exactly I had landed there. She took my arm with her cold tiny fingers and helped me up gently. I looked myself up and down and I felt sweat all over me. I could feel that my face was agitated from all the salty tears that had wandered down my face.

'Mia did you understand what I told you?' she asked.

I just nodded. I was not really present. I was still in the place I had been in my dreams. The place I had been before. In my black hole, where nothing mattered. Where there were no feelings, were there were no obligations. Where I was free and did not need to worry. I just lay back on my bed and waited for the time to pass without forgetting to go to the doctor's office. I knew I had to stay awake otherwise I would fall into my black hole again, forget and miss the time. So, I stared at the wall. I tried to imagine what I would draw on the wall. What I would want the next patient in this room to see. But I could not figure out anything. But it at least had relaxed my mind for a bit. It was 14.50 and time had passed quickly. I think time in my head passes faster than in real life. Some carer whose name I could never remember had come to get me to escort me to Dr. Splean's office. In the office it was the usual. I was getting more and more sure that this guy did not know anything. He just asked questions and it seemed as if he asked as slowly as possible, just to pass time. Maybe just to make it seem as if he was actually working. Well, I don't know. And I don't care. Days passed in the clinic. It felt like I had never been anywhere else in my entire life. Alyssa would not give me any information about Alice, and I had not seen Mike. It felt like my life had gotten even more lonely than ever. It was like hours were just passing in my mind but not in real life. it was not normal. I did not even know which day it was, which month it was, which year. Every minute was the same. I had even started to forget to eat, which was out of the norm for me. My whole life was spinning around; the questions I had to myself and to others, and the regret. They were my worst enemies; well I was my worst enemy. I did not understand. One day my hunger was so great that my mind decided it would be a good idea to eat something. I wandered over to the cafeteria, probably so slowly that I was close to standing still. In the cafeteria I could not believe my eyes. It took me quite a while to realize that it was Mike standing in front of me. In line for food. I had been searching him for weeks and now I had not even noticed him at first sight. I just can't ... how did that happen to me? How did I miss him? I had recalled his appearance one million times in my head. I had imagined his eyes day and night. I had tried to repaint a picture in my head of him with every tiny detail. And now he was here casually standing, right in front of me, just trying to mind his own business and I had not recognised him. Had he noticed me and was just ignoring me?

'What can I get you?' one of the lunch ladies asked.

I was not prepared to answerer her question and just snapped, 'Can't I just have some peace here or what?' at her even though she had not done anything. I was quite embarrassed after but what did I care? I had just found the man who could answerer the majority of my questions that were floating in my head. Maybe I could start thinking straight again after this. Whatever *this* was? But I had lost time and he had moved on in the line. How could I have lost him that fast? The lunch lady was staring at me, straight into my eyes. She scooped a big thing of some muck that was meant for the patients with no teeth. It was probably her revenge. But my hunger had faded. There was only one important thing right now. I was determined. Now was my chance. Now or never. Here we go. I walked through the cafeteria balancing the tray, which was not so easy with crutches, believe me. I took a look at every table. Just examining everyone to find the clear ocean-blue eyes I so desperately wanted to meet mine. And there he was sitting outside on the bench where me and Alice had always sat. My determination started to wane as I got closer. As I was slowly approaching, I started to get scared, anxious. I was not sure if this encounter was going to change my life forever. I turned back for a second but then continued my path towards him. He saw me or I at least think he did cause he looked at me and just observed me carefully. His eyes were peered open. He did not even wink once, his irises were directed directly towards me. That's when I saw my tray make a dive for the ground. Everything scattered everywhere. A huge mess.

I saw nurses coming. I knew I was in trouble. I moved faster than I ever had with my crutches, I needed to talk to Mike before I got into trouble. And he got up from the bench and placed his food down beside him. It felt like everything was happening in slow motion, but it was happening. I approached him. It felt like every step was a marathon. When we met face to face, he said nothing just gave me a look and stroked my shoulder, leaving a warm and cosy feeling where he touched. But before I could collect myself and say something, I was surrounded by two nurses questioning what I was doing. Making Mike sit back down. All I could hear was mumbling and the ladies faces looking at mine, waiting for a response. Everything was becoming unclear. I just heard things but did not understand what they were saying. Mike got up again, probably against the will of the nurse and just came so close to me, closer than before. Really, so close I felt his breath getting hotter and hotter as he got closer and closer. His lips met mine. And the world turned black.

I woke up in my bed. I tried to get up, but I could not. It was like I was paralyzed. I was stuck where I was. I could not go anywhere. I checked twice that I was not strapped to the bed. The door was shut which probably meant I was locked in as well. I just wanted answers. I let out a scream in the hope It would minimize my anger. But all that it did was make me aware that I had never left my room. Because the clock was still showing 11.30 which meant that either that what just happened never happened, or I was going crazy, or 24 hours had passed. I could not settle with any of the ideas. They were all stupid. But then for once in a long time my questions were answered. Alyssa had come in and remarked that I should go to lunch. She had not seen me there in a while. She would have reacted differently if the thing with Mike had happened. On one hand I was relieved but on the other I was back to zero of getting what I wanted out of Mike. Whatever that was? I went to lunch, even though it felt like I had already been there once today. I looked everywhere for Mike but unlike in my apparent dream he was nowhere to be seen, not in sight. I could feel the disappointment rush though my veins. I just ate and left. Back to my room to spend a whole lot of time doing nothing except escaping into my black hole waiting for better times which would never come for me.

'Mia?', a deep calm voice said. So familiar but never heard.

I turned my head and there standing in front of me was Mike. His eyes seemed to be mirrors, they were shining so beautifully. I was really obsessed with his eyes. I could see the reflection of the floor in his eyes. He sat down on the bed that had been unoccupied since the day he had been strapped to it. What was I going to do? Mia, ask what you need to know. But before I could Mike spoke up.

'Mia what happened in the laundry room should not have happened. It was not right of me. Neither should lots of other things that have happened to you. Unfortunately, it is in my nature. I don't know why. And all I want to say is sorry even though I am not sorry for everything that happened. It does not matter how hard I try but somethings I just can't be sorry for, but I know I should and that is why I am, sort of.'

Was he being sincere or was everything just dreamt up by me again? No, this was real. It had to be because never ever could have I imagined this situation ever happening. It was really as if I had met Mike again, met once more the personality he had had in university. Maybe therapy was good for him, unlike for me. Wonder what they had figured out about his trauma from the apparent witnessed murder that had apparently happened.

Minutes went by while I just looked at him trying to sort my thoughts, trying to figure out what I should say or do. But in the end my question was not thought through, just intuitive.

'Why were we not together in university? Why did you never ask me out properly, like you just messed around with me? Why?'

I asked the thing I was probably not really worried about, but I guess my brain was.

'Well, when I was younger, I avoided dating because I was scared of being hurt. I did not want to lose the only true friend I had ever had. Who had introduced me to so much in life. But then later on I could not because I had started really wanting one thing, which was money and power at any cost, and I needed you to get it. I know it sounds stupid but all I saw then was money and I still do mostly.'

Could he start making sense please?

Mike continued. 'Look I am a mean person. I like seeing people suffer even the ones I love most. I just lose my control over myself and then all I can think about is money. Even though over the years I have made billions. It does not matter to me, but I want to change. I just can't. I have only had joy in two things in my life so far. Money and then when I started seeing you. You are the one who made university amazing. If you had not been there, I would have started illegal stuff much earlier, and I had not started because I was afraid of losing you. The only way I could soothe myself was with money and violence. I have so much aggression inside of me and the only way of getting rid of it was by hurting others.'

My eyes were more open than they have ever been. I just could not believe my senses. Was Mike talking here to me like a decent human being? I just did not understand.

'Mia, I fell for you a long time ago and I just did not know how to deal with it. And I wanted you but then there was money which was like a magnet towards me. It was like an addiction, and it still is. I just can't leave it alone, it's part of me. And all the stuff I have gotten myself into I cannot get out of. I have done too many things. I have sent too many people to prison, I have smuggled dugs, I have sold things on the black market. I have trafficked people and worst of all I have hurt you. Now I know I have wounded you inside and outside and I know that I partially enjoyed it, but I find joy in punishing others. Perhaps it's because I should be punished but I am not. All I want to say is sorry. It's the only thing I can say to this situation.'

I did not know what else to do, what to say, what I should think.

'Mia, please just forgive me or accept what I am saying. I just need it to live on. And when you get out of here, I will give you back your papers, so you will be able to go live a more or less normal life. I think I have done enough damage and I am starting to lose my joy in punishing you for things I did or do. I am realizing it was not fair. I should be the one locked up in here not you.'

We sat in silence, me staring into his eyes, imagining jumping into them like into the chilly ocean. I felt the sea breeze, smelt the slight scent of seaweed and I could feel the salt in the air, the sand surrounding my feet.

I burst out, 'What happened in the laundry room?'

'I could not resist Mia, I have had feelings for you for a long time and I saw you there I could not stop myself and I did not want to. I had lost all my fears in that moment, and it had not occurred to me how wrong it was. Almost everything I do is immoral, but I can't self-control.'

He came closer. A lot closer and again the feelings from that night got replicated. Mike was all over me. I could feel him, everywhere on and in me. More questions were formed in my head, but I could not ask them. But beside Mike, I could forget them for a bit even though he was the one who the most questions revolved around. But I felt safe even if this was the man who had almost killed me in my dreams, the man who had ordered a man to shoot me, the man who treated me cruelly. But it was like he was none of that, well in that moment. I could feel my eyelids falling as he stroked my head with his warm hands, the affection would spread from my head all the way down to my toes. I fell asleep. I had not slept that well in a long time. As I reached for him when I woke up, he was nowhere. I was reaching into the empty air just catching molecules of carbon dioxide. He was gone. Just gone, had left me here alone. With even more questions, new questions. I wanted to know not just the Mike from the past but the Mike from the present, it seemed like he knew me, but I did not know him anymore or never had known him. Or I knew multiple hims.

Another three days passed. It was like most of the time I had spent in the clinic. I figured out that I had been in the clinic for forty-seven days, well I had asked Alyssa. I also figured out that Alice was still in somewhere between conscious and unconscious. When Alyssa had come to tell me that I was going to be released tomorrow I did not know if I should be excited or sad or anxious or afraid. The emotions were too overwhelming and I would have wanted to just sink into oblivion. It had been my goal to get out of this place as soon as possible, as soon as I had gotten here, and now the day had come. But what would I do in the real world? How would I ever be able to figure out the things from Mike if I was not here anymore? How could I leave with Alice in this state? The more the hours passed the more I thought of how my life would be on the outside. I had begged to see Alice before I went, and Alyssa had half-promised me that I would be able to and that I did not need to worry because I would need to come back to the clinic four more times in the first two months that I was out just to check if everything was going ok. That is how I found myself crying beside Alice's bed, kissing her forehead, telling her a bunch of stuff, crying more and then being dragged out with eyes full of tears. I never saw Mike and I did not want to ask Alyssa about him. I was given some conventional clothes – I wondered why they didn't give me back the clothes I had once put inside a plastic box, but whatever. They had probably dematerialised by now. Additionally, I was given my passport, however that had landed in the clinic, a bank card to an account I did not own, probably the work of Mike. Well, it had to be. I walked out of the clinic, and I felt like a new person. I was going to leave this behind me and go make myself a decent life. I walked and walked. Till I reached the bus station, well it was not that far though it felt like it had taken forever to get there. I took the bus to Charleston. I knew the town because when I was around ten years old, I had visited it with my family. And I had thought it was better to go somewhere I knew even the slightest bit. The bus ride went faster than I had expected. I watched the trees outside, the other cars, and was just stuck in my head with all my thoughts. Just letting my mind roam, letting it do whatever it wanted. I was finally free. I could do what I want. I arrived and got out of the bus, smelling the exhausts from the cars, the sewage, the general city smell. But to me it smelt good. It smelt like a new place. A new beginning. I just sat down and watched life take place. I watched mothers with their children walking down the streets with groceries in their hands. I watched men smoke their cigarettes, I watched shop owners clean their front windows. I watched taxi drivers honk as they got impatient. Simply I watched everything. I had spotted a bank after I had seen a child run after their dog which had taken off. I decided to get up and headed towards the bank. The banker looked at me in surprise when he told me I had a million dollars on my account. Mike was rich, and that he had given me money meant a lot. Money was like his number one priority. And he had given me the thing which was worth the most to him. I just walked out. I just had to scream when I got out. It was a scream of joy, of shock. I had never had this much money. I would never need to worry about going broke again, never. It was starting to get dark, the streetlights started to turn on as the sun was setting. I was going to need to find a place to stay. I found a hotel nearby and booked a room with my full credit card. The pin was easy it was the same as the one Mike had on his locker. I wondered how he had known that I would know that. But to me it just had seemed logical. The next few days I spent most of my time thinking. I had applied for a job at the same pharmaceutical company I had worked at before. I bought an apartment in New York. I wanted to go back. I loved the town despite the memories. The rest of the time I tried to find Mike somehow.

LOSS

I made my way back to the clinic for my so-called check-up with Dr. Splean. I was excited because I thought I would have a chance to see Alice. I walked into the clinic like a different person. I was an ex-patient and the thought of that felt so good. I was more confident, more content. I saw something in life. The past was the past. I would always have regrets but ya. I went to Dr.Splean's office accompanied by a nurse. He made me fill out a question-naire and asked a few things. Then I was off looking for Alyssa to find Alice even though I was not just supposed to wander around the clinic.

'Mia, you know you shouldn't be here!' Alyssa exclaimed.

'I just want to see Alice. Please let me, you know she is impor-tant to me. I'm begging you.' The look on Alyssa's face changed she stayed silent and then gulped so loud I could almost feel my own saliva going down my throat.

'Mia, Alice died a few days ago. She did not make it. I am so sorry.'

My lips started to tremble. I could feel the tears coming, and they did. I slid down to the ground, beat.

'I am so sorry. She died two days ago. She was very weak. She wanted to die ... she killed herself. But she left you a letter. There was nothing we could do. I am so sorry.'

'Dear Mia, I know you would be back here for your check-up, so I wanted to end this before too many feelings flood-ed me. Please don't worry about me. I was getting bet-ter but then as soon as they took me off of the feeding tube everything went downhill. Faster than it had ever gone. They basically plugged me back in and I just knew as soon as I was off of it, I would do the same to myself

*again. I just can't handle my anorexic thoughts anymore
so I think it is the right decision to just leave this world.
I won't need to deal with any of the problems anymore
and no one will have to deal with me. I cannot handle it
anymore. I am hurting myself to an extent where I have
nothing more to live for. I do not see the point anymore
and I just want to end my pain. I know you will be mad
at yourself that you did not do anything but please don't
be. I am doing it for myself it was my decision. You have
no fault at all. Sooner or later, it would happen anyway.
I also think my death will devastate you and my family, but I just think without me their all of them and you
will have some weight off their shoulders. You are the
one who definitely needs weight lifted off your shoulder. Mia you are a great person and it's not your fault
what happened in the past. You cannot change it either.
I don't know the whole story but I can just imagine. But
I am so glad that you told me part of your story, that you
opened up to me. Please just start new. And live happi-
ly, you can still make something great out of your life,
I am sure. And I know you might be sad now but don't
be, just forget me I am not worth remembering. Just focus on yourself, don't ruin yourself like I did. I know you
won't cause you are soo much stronger. There is nothing
that can hurt you now. There is so much more to say but
putting emotions into words is not my thing and my energy won't allow me to write more. I will always have a
special place in my heart for you.*

Why? I cried with reddened eyes. She was one of the few people in my life that I actually cared about and now she was gone,
like everything else. Just gone. Disappeared. Never to be found
again. And she was wrong that nothing could hurt me now because exactly this hurt me. I thought she was getting better.
Before I had left she was eating and she was still ok. How did
everything go downhill so fast.

Alyssa had sat down beside me in the hallway. I just stared at the wall with the hope I would wake up from this nightmare and still be in elementary school. Maybe that would be a bit of a harsh dream for a ten-year-old, high school seemed more appropriate. Unfortunately, that was not the case. It was real. More real than I could bear. I think Alyssa did not dare touch me since I was always so bitchy to her when she had stroked my shoulder in the clinic. But they had just stuck me in this place without my consent so how could I be nice? I was holding the letter, reading it through several times, to be sure of what I had read and that it was the truth. I did not want to believe it, I did not want to. This was not fair to me nor to her. The letter ripped in half, drenched in tears, my hands clutching it tensely. The paper started to rip and fall apart. I tried to fix it, it was all I had. I could just see the running ink that was getting smeared all across the paper and my hands. I cried for two hours until some other nurse had lost patience with me and Alyssa was told she should take me to my appointment and stop pitting and puttering. I did not listen to Dr. Splean for a minute. All that filled my mind was Alice. How had she killed herself? Why, I just did not understand. Had I not seen when she was feeling so bad? Was I soo in my own head, had I just been full of myself, just been a bitch and not seen the pain she was suffering? I could never forgive myself. She had gotten me to open up, have a bit of joy again in life and what had I done for her? Absolutely nothing. I had only talked about myself. I had thought my force feeding would be a good thing, but it had probably set her back. I did not understand her illness to the full extent, but I could never ever forgive myself. Somehow, I managed to get through the appointment with Dr. Splean. I rode the bus 'home'. I just cried the whole time once I had gotten back to my hotel room I had been staying in since I had left the clinic, I had gone to the grocery store, bought a family sized mint and chocolate chip ice cream bucket, sat down and just spooned it in while I cried into it, which gave it a salty taste, but taste did not matter, I just wanted to sink into nothingness. I had money, I had a passport, I had an education, I was physically healthy kind of, but it felt like I had nothing at all. I had no more passion, no more empathy if I had ever had any. I was empty inside. I wish I could be happy I had gotten out of this dark stage of my life, I was free but I was miserable. I could as well of been gone like Alice, but I wasn't. I was here, and she was gone. It would have been better if she had been here, and I was gone. She deserved life more than I did, but I could not bring myself ever to kill myself. I would always think about it, but I could not do it and that showed that Alice was stronger than me. I was weak and broken. Inside and out. My face was sticky and all salty and I was just done. I could not get up, I had no power, no desire to do anything. I lay on my floor for the whole day looking at the ceiling, not even moving an inch. I probably looked like a doll. Well, not a doll, more like a dead person or a Halloween dummy. I could hear my phone ringing and I had no clue who the hell it could be, who would know the number to call and who would even call me. Who even knew I existed anymore? I did not understand. It rang and rang but then stopped. I thought maybe somebody had just dialled the wrong number but shortly after it started ringing again. Maybe it's just a coincidence. Things like this happen, don't they? After the sixth time I couldn't kid myself that it was just a twist of fate and managed to lift my body from the floor and walk to the night table where the phone sat. I grabbed the receiver, and it was if I had never picked up a phone before. I just said nothing, no hello, no is anyone there, no hello my name is Mia. I said nothing and waited as if I expected the person on the line just to know that I picked up. I then heard a breath on the other side of the line. I was nervous, as if it was a new technology. I had not used a phone in forever. I jumped a little when I heard a very familiar voice, probably the only voice that was familiar to me. Mike. Well, who else could it have been? He was basically the only person who maybe cared a bit or he at least knew who I was.

'Mia, I wanted to ask you if they gave you a credit card when you left the clinic. It's a bank account under your name. The code to the card is something that you can probably guess, the locker code. I know you used to know it better than me.'

'Whh …,' but the phone line was cut off. Why, did I always need to question everything? Many people on this planet would not say anything if someone random put a million on their bank account. But I cared. Mike was not some random nobody, he was somebody I knew so well, though did not know at all. But at least I had guessed the code right and had one million. But what did that matter if I did not want to do anything with it? It could be one-hundred and it would be worth the same to me. It did not matter; money did not matter to me. I was not Mike Money was worth money but nothing more. Relationships with people were worth something much more, a more valuable currency. I know me saying this is odd because I cut out soo many relations, pushed soo many people away, acted like a bitch so many times, ignored others when they were feeling unwell and took everything and everyone for granted. But I just knew that relationships were worth more or they were at least worth more to me now. Now when I did not have any. I was alone.

NEW BEGINNING

There was mail slid in through the opening in the door. I went to grab it. I had gotten the job in New York. I could not believe it, but it did not make me happy. I had lost too much. It was just a small excitement not more than if I won one dollar in the lottery. It did not seem to matter. But I found myself moving to New York the following week. I could say I was going with the flow, maybe. Mike had also sent me my driver's license and my birth certificate and some things that I had had at the factory. I had bought a car and I found myself driving to New York in the car I always wanted, to the apartment I soo loved, to the job I had been so passionate about. But I did not feel any positive emotions. I was just sad. I did not know about what exactly, but I was sad about everything a bit – everything I had seemed worthless. If I had looked at a picture of myself twenty years ago, I probably would have thought: Wow! You managed to buy your beloved apartment, Wow! you got the car that you always wanted. You probably have finished developing the drug to treat cancer, you are probably making amazing money and you probably can go out with your friends every weekend. You are probably a better person than I am today and have learned soo much over the years. You might be living with a loving boyfriend. You must have a fulfilled life. But all I had was the car, the apartment and money – nothing else and the things that I wanted so badly were so far away. Happiness. Joy. I wanted to forget and stop regretting. I had nothing at all. I just could not anymore. I lay down on my bed and waited for it to be Monday so that I would need to get ready for work. But it seemed like the night would never end. I was thinking and thinking, my brain could not take a break. I still had soo many questions, and I just could not start anew. I could not leave my past behind me. I would always wonder how it would have been if it had been different. I would never be able to forgive myself and I would always live full of the regrets and in the past. I could just not live in the present anymore. I was too weak. My mind had a mind of its own. But to my relief the alarm went off, it was 6.30. Finally, I could get up and hopefully think of other things.

I made my way to the lab of the pharmaceutical company. It was not like I remembered. The building was bigger and there were new buildings. They used to be just plain brick buildings but now they were modern concrete structures with large windows looking into the offices. The labs were at the back side of the building or at least they used to be. I walked in through the revolving doors which led to the reception. I could of spun through a few times – I did not want to face people, but I had to seem not mental. There was a middle-aged woman sitting there. She introduced herself as Katherine. She made me fill out a few forms and sign them then she gave me some lab clothes and led me to the changing rooms that were in front of the lab. I wondered if anyone I had worked with still worked here. I got changed while Katherine waited for me. She showed me the lunchroom and the offices where some of the scientists worked, then she led me to the lab where I was going to work.

'When we looked at your application, we realized that you had already once worked here. When we were looking into your archived file, we found out that you had been working on a drug for cancer treatment. A colleague of yours had tried to complete it but just couldn't so it was just put off and we worked on other things, but since you are back, we decided that you should continue your work, because from what I have heard you were really close to developing it. The company has given you this whole lab and two interns to help you. This is a first in my experience. You must have been a special chemist before you left. Enjoy your day and if you need anything just come to the front desk.'

I felt like I had been thrown into cold water, I did not remember what I was doing, all of this was years ago. I remembered all the convincing it took me to be able to start developing the drug.

First as extra work hours then on a few weekdays and finally it was my full-time occupation. The lab had not changed much – there was some new equipment, and the tables were a different colour. But I was thrilled that I could go on working on my life's work. But this still did not make me happy. Before Katherine had left, she mentioned the names of the interns, Callie and Brian. They seemed very shy and had only shyly said hello and nice to meet you. But they seemed like intelligent people or at least they looked like dorks. I was kinda overwhelmed. I could not exactly remember where I had left off it was such a long time ago. I wondered if they knew that I had been in jail or if somehow that was erased to. I did not know. Oh, and not to forget the mental facility. Callie had brought me a map full of notes.

'They told us that you would probably need this.'

It was all the notes, all the numbers I had written down when I was trying to develop the drug. I practically hugged it. Eerie, but whatever.

'Me and Brian already needed to copy it all so that all of it would be online, but we thought you might want to keep working with paper and don't worry we can copy it onto the computer afterwards.'

'Sounds great.'

After just a few minutes of studying my papers it seemed like I had just worked on it yesterday. Everything was present again. I started telling them how they should set up and we started mixing and boiling and analysing. I was in my place doing something I liked but I still did not love it. Or maybe I wasn't letting myself enjoy it. Maybe I did not want to be happy. Maybe I could not be happy.

By the end of the day, we had just done a few tests and had not gotten much further. The two students had gone home, and I was left alone in the lab. Even though my workday was over I stayed there. I wanted to test a few more things. My work had been put on hold for years, I needed to catch up. That's how I ended up falling asleep on the stone floor of the lab at around two o'clock in the morning. The time had just passed without me even realizing. While I was sleeping, I had dreamt that I was back working in the factory, although most of the dream was filled with dark memories. I dreamt about the times when all the factory workers would sit together around a fire outside and we had tried to be happy. This was a rare occasion at the factory. We would warm ourselves around the fire, tell each other stories and dream about the times when had not been there. I would never forget the time when Fergus finally told me about his past. I was touched, I was taken back. He had needed money because his brother was being accused of a murder that he had not committed. They were a poor family and Fergus needed money for a lawyer to help prove the innocence of his three-year younger brother. He had tried to work extra hours; he had tried to put together all his savings; he had tried getting bank loans, and lending money. But nothing was enough, time was starting to get tight, really tight, so he saw no other way. It had all started with dealing drugs on the street. But after he had made enough money for the lawyer the drug cartel would not let him go – he was stuck. They had threatened to kill his fiancée if he left, so he saw no other choice but to stay. He was too afraid to talk to anyone about it and had just stayed, but they always made him do more, not just drug dealing. He was under their control every second and their control grew stronger, along with their demands. But he followed like a puppy dog, too scared was he of the consequences if he didn't. He ended up smuggling drugs, killing four people, and going to prison for things he did not do nor had control over. When he got out of prison, he had refused to work with them and just like that his beloved one-year-old daughter went missing the next day. He had raged, he had fought back with everything he could. But there was no point they were so much more powerful than he was. He was given a choice to be killed or to come and work in the factory. That is how he and his wife had found themselves in a factory in the middle of a forest working harder than any human should and being treated like slaves. Anyway, they had accepted that they were going to work in the factory for the rest of their lives. They were always trying to be nice and kind. I admired them and when I saw Fergus sometimes, I would forget all the horrible things he had done, like I could not even imagine him doing any of those things. Every time I tried to imagine how he killed people my heart would ache cause he was such a good person. He would never hurt a fly. But he could do it cause it was to save himself and his family.

I could feel someone tugging on my arm. At first, I thought it was part of my dream but then as it got stronger I could make out Katherine's voice. I knew I did not want to open my eyes. But I did. She must have thought I was a complete weirdo but who cared? Well, I did care slightly. I did not feel like losing my job today. I wanted to finish this drug then they could fire me. The idea for the pill was genius, or that is at least what I thought. It was supposed to act like a leukocyte, to be exact, a natural killer cell but in a more efficient way. These kinds of lively pills would be able to recognise cancer cells immediately and not just kill one-by-one but all at once. I thought it was so smart. The pills were going to be kind of face organisms that did everything that white blood cells did just more precise, they would only phagocyte cancer cells and destroy their uncontrollable multiplying DNA.

To my surprise Katherine was very calm, and it seemed like this was not something unusual. However, she did ask me from now on to work in the normal hours and not to stay here all night. Maybe others had done the same, maybe others were as irrational as I was or maybe they did not have a social life because they were nerds. But that was unlikely. Maybe they did not want a social life so that is why they did not have one. I did not have one either, but I wanted it so desperately. Katherine left me in the lab but came back after a while carrying a coffee and a croissant in her hand.

'Here you go, and please just look like you did not spend the night here when Brian and Callie arrive. I would appreciate it.'

She left. She was actually the only one who had talked to me during the time I had been here but I had never talked to her, I could not even remember if I had said more than my name when

I had arrived. Oh well the two interns had introduced them self but we did not talk much, they were two very shy quiet kids. But it seemed to work this way. To be fair it was only my second day. I got kinda cleaned up in the bathroom and then went back into the lab to continue before the other two came.

The day passed quickly. I got along with Brian and Callie. They were friendly and helpful, so I was happy. Well, happy enough, but I was still not really happy. I wanted a life I did not have. When I got back to my apartment, I sat at my kitchen table and all I did was put my head in my hands and cry. I wanted to erase my memory. Why had I ever met Mike? Why had I ever met Alice? All the relationships and friendships I have had with people are literally for the trash. I ruined all of them. The images of Alice dying came back and that's where I was; I was imagining being in her body. How would it have felt to kill herself? Did it hurt? Was it relieving? Was it pleasurable? Had she started regretting it half-way through? Would I regret it if I would simply try to kill myself right now? Would that not solve all my problems? No more worries, no more fears, all gone, and I can get away from this horrible planet where everything is unfair and doesn't happen for a reason. There is no reason behind anything, everything just happens. All that we humans are here for is to eat, drink, reproduce and then die, nothing more. Not to invent crazy things, to question every existing thing. But that was the only thing I did, I did not do the things I should. Well, partially, a bit. I did some of the things I should but definitely not all. I wanted to go away. Like I was getting nowhere with my drug development. There was not even a point in developing this drug cause there was no point in life, so why should I make something that would have the power of healing people. I had nothing that gave me joy in life, I had nothing to look forward to. I did not understand myself. There was no one that cared about me. Well there was Mike, but he did not count; he was out of my thoughts at the moment but he brought me the most worries and questions. Not even those answers would please me. I could not even think of a thing that would make me joyful. I was not even addicted to food so I could not even turn to that. Otherwise, I would buy all the junk out there and stuff my face with sugar and fat all weekend. But that was not an option for me. Food did not bring me joy anymore. It was like a necessity nothing more. Mia what is wrong with you? What is wrong with this fake world you live in? Everything has no sense, everything is worth nothing. There is just no point anymore. No point in life. Everything just sucks. Just imagine if all the problems would disappear, no more worries, no more things I would need to think about. No more things that would bring me troubles. Everything could just fade away. Maybe this could bring me joy, seeing myself go. Seeing all my problems go away one by one or all at once. Never to come again. If I was not here on earth, I could not have any problems here anymore. Life would be done but better done than suffering from it. Or not? Mia, just gosh! You're not going to kill yourself. Think about all the people you're going to save with your drug. Life is worthless though so why should I save them, why me? I was useless on this planet, I wanted to leave. I had no family that would suffer if I were gone. Mike would not matter if he would suffer. I had suffered from him enough in my life. Would anyone even notice if I would just strangle myself right now. Would it even be a big deal? I could set everything up so that it looked like I had had a heart attack or fallen asleep in the bathtub. Then whoever would notice would just be sad and not even know that I committed suicide. If someone ever came searching for me. But could I do it, would I be strong enough to kill myself? Could I bring myself to do it or would I fail it again? Would the fear of I don't know what start creeping up? Start stopping me, limiting me? I started filling the bath with water, I put on music, cleaned up. It was supposed to look like everything was fine in my life. I even booked some flight to Paris so that they might think I don't know what. I printed them out and set them down on the kitchen table. This was suspicious. No, it was not. I printed some other things from Paris and laid them all over the table. I ran to the bathroom, hoping my bath was not overflowing yet.

It was fine. I undressed and placed all my clothes neatly beside the bathtub. I put in a toe to check the temperature and slowly I slid into the tub. The lukewarm water felt nice as it touched every part of my body. I was determined to get this over and done with. Every second on this earth was worthless. I held my breath and dived under. I closed my mouth and slowly I started running out of oxygen. It felt good but then the pain became immense. I was not sure if I could do it. I tried to think about all my problems, everything I would not need to deal with anymore. I tried so hard. But I was too weak. I had no control over my actions and my head rose above the water again. My lungs longing for air, me breathing heavily and fast, panting. I felt myself almost catching the air with my hands to stuff it down my lungs. After I had recovered, I just sat there, questioning myself. Why was I not able to do it? Why could I have not just held my breath a bit longer, endured a tiny bit more. I was weaker than weak. Alice had done it. But here I was and again I could not do it. I got out of the fucking bath and went to look at my flights to Paris I had purchased. What the hell was I supposed to do with them now? I had bought tickets for six hundred and forty-three dollars. Paris return flight. Should I go to Paris? No! What was the point? Why the hell would I want to go to Paris? I don't want to go to Paris. It's all so touristy, too fancy schmancy. No thank you, I am good without that. Well, a few hundred did not matter when I had hundreds of thousands. I had enough money anyway. But I did not want to waste it, nevertheless. I sat there at my table staring at the random stuff I had printed out. But my mind had drifted far from Paris, thinking of Paris would have been present compared to what I was thinking. I had imagined my death several times, tried to make new suicide plans, tried to figure out how Alice did it, how many others had done it before me. Then I had gone back to the factory in my memories. But this time I was going through all the time I had wasted there, after work I had just done nothing unless I was not asked a million times by the other to join them. In the beginning I had spent far more time with them but as time had passed the more I had shut myself away from all of them. I did not even know why, when I thought of it. It had just happened for no reason. Or maybe there was a reason, but I did not know it. The more I analysed the more I recognized I had been doing the same, basically my whole life. With my family, with my friends with everyone. Why was I like this? No wonder I had no relationships with people. What the hell was wrong with me, did I have like zero social skills or like negative social skills? I don't understand, why do I gotta be like this? I don't want to, not the slightest bit. I was ruining my one life and the lives of others. My plan B was not suicide, it had to be plan A. It was the only plan. The only plan that would work. I got up out of my chair and knocked it down at the same time, I made my way to the cleaning cupboard, took out everything that was in there and mixed myself a glass with the blue and green liquids. It smelt quite pleasant. I stared gulping it down but after just two gulps I threw up all over. I threw up over and over again till all I was throwing up was a kind of foam.

So here we are once again, again I had not managed. I was weak. How was I ever going to manage to just do it, really. Like how hard could it be? I tried to strangle myself but all the damage that it did was a few red marks and not more. I tried a second time but the same thing again. I could not withstand it long enough. I was starting to really get frustrated. What if I just jumped out of the window. No, then everyone would see, no thank you. I didn't want that much attention, even if I was dead.

THE END, OR SOMETHING LIKE THAT

The day in the lab was a day full of theatre. I felt like I was a Hollywood actor. I had to pretend that everything was fine, that I was fine. That I was doing my job. Well, I was. But my brain did not have any capacity to think about this stupid drug. I was not getting anywhere with it. Not even a bit. I hated it when I worked on something but got no outcome, or basically stayed on the same step and not climb any higher or even be going backwards. I was so happy when the two interns left because they had been bugging me a bit today. I wanted my peace and quiet, I did not want constant questions. I did not want someone asking every second, what can we do? What are you doing? Like holy fuck just let me do one step without you. I did not know what to do with the two of them. As they left, I had gotten out the old notebook and sat down and started to just look through it, reading what I had written, questioning if my intelligence had decreased. Maybe due to the chemicals in the factory. On one page I discovered that there was a handwriting which did not belong to me. Whose was it, when had this been written? For God's sake Mia maybe just read what it says then you probably will understand.

0795432721, Tuesday 21.30, experiment 73.

What on earth was this supposed to mean? Had this been written before I had left my position here or while I was rotting at the factory? What did I even care? It was just a few numbers and two words. Did I have to make such a big deal? Could I just not leave it alone and not question it? No, I couldn't. That was just not me. I was incapable of such an action. I looked up if it could be a phone number. But all that popped up on the internet was some weird part on an online shop that had that item number. Then I came across a site in a language I did not understand one bit. So, I went back to browse through other sites. I also came across a company, which sold tractors, which had similar numbers in their name. But there was nothing useful, nothing that actually meant something, well maybe something did, and I was just too stupid to know it. That could have been the case. But I was the stupid one here. Why was I looking up a phone number, surely it was not? But I did not give up. I had gone to the front desk and looked for a phone book. Katherina had gone home along with everyone else and contrary to what she had told me this morning I was still here hanging around, getting my brain messed up by one line someone else had written in my notes. But I had given up following the system. Maybe I could do something that would get me sent back to prison – there I could get one of the inmates to kill me in return for some money. I am sure that would somehow work. But how the hell was I going to do that? Mia, just look for that damm phone book! Concentrate on one thing, then you can move to the next. I went through the whole reception desk. I pulled out every door with force, hit them closed with my hips, but I could not find anything. Did they not have any phone books these days? Like those things are the most practical things ever invented so why the hell would you get rid of them? I did not understand. I should start understanding instead of not understanding the whole time. Gosh Mia.

Why was I like this? I did not want to be like this. I did not like myself like this. I did not like myself at all. I looked at the number again and realized that the prefix was not American. After a bit more internet research I figured out that it was a Swiss phone number. But that did not bring me any further.

After a few more internet pages, I finally managed to give up investigating and made my way home. I think I was the only human being that was sad that the weekend was coming up. What the hell was I supposed to do? Was I supposed to try and kill myself again or what was the plan? I had no more plans. I just wanted to fade away. I kicked the pavement as I made my way from the bus stop to my apartment. I used to love this place so much more. I went up the stairs and force fed myself some crackers that were the opposite of delicious. More like disgusting. To me at least. I lay down on my bed and started glaring at the ceiling again, wondering what I should do with my life I honestly did not know. I really did not know. End it maybe. I started to giggle. I did not even know why. Why was I laughing at my suicidal thoughts? Was my life such a joke?

I heard someone knock. That must be for my neighbour, who had a social life, unlike me. Who had relationships with people, unlike me. But I heard the knock again and this time it was louder and more aggressive. Was it the same person, was it someone else? Were they knocking on my door? Was everything just an illusion? Was it all happening in my imagination? My uncertainty faded when I heard the knock become more repetitive, aggressive and along with that, louder. It would not stop. I was also clear that someone was knocking at my door now. I had moved from my bed and had put my ear against the door to ensure I was not fooling myself. It was someone was knocking on my door, there was no doubt. I reached for the handle. And unlike someone at the wrong door, standing there in front of me, was Mike. He must be at the right door. Must. He just came in without saying a word, shut the door behind him and walked to my kitchen table. He picked up the flight tickets and the other paper stuff that was on the table and had a thorough look over it, before he turned his head to me. I was standing in the hallway, well in the mud room basically. He just waited for my eyes to meet his. As if he knew that that would trigger something inside of me. Unfortunately, he was not completely wrong. It felt like my leg was working without my consciousness. I started moving towards Mike. I sat down across from him at my kitchen table. When my bottom hit the woven chair he said, 'Mia I love you, but I can't love you.'

Now what the fuck was that supposed to mean? In those few words there were one million emotions that did not go together, and they were contradictory. Like really. Mike, what was wrong with you? What was wrong with both of us? Was I worse than him? Mia did you not tell yourself once not to compare yourself to him. Just control yourself, nothing more. He reached for my hand under the table and squeezed, almost squished it tight, so I had no chance of escaping, but after a few seconds I did not even want to escape. I wanted my hand to stay right there; it felt like it belonged right there and nowhere else. I think he felt that the tension I initially had were absorbed by his hand, so the grip he had around my hand softened and became a lot looser. My hand was now in its perfect environment. It was like my hand was just made for his, they fit together perfectly. Like a key into a lock. He just held it and looked me in the eyes like he was trying to tell me something without saying it. Unfortunately, I was not telepathic. Once again, I would have had an opportunity to ask the questions to which I so desperately wanted answers but I just kinda did not want to. I had not had a moment like this in a long time, more like ever. I just felt good, almost happy, and I did not want to let go of those feelings. I did not. I did not know how long it would last.

'Mia please don't leave me here waiting for you to tell me off, tell me what you are thinking. I can't just sit here and try to imagine what is going on in your head. Because I can't read you. You are you, you know what I mean. Please just say something,' he said.

There were a million things I could say. I just did not know what. I wanted to be loved by people, but I did not know if these people included Mike. Just be fast, you can't let him wait. Well, yes I can, but I am not sure if I want to.

'Look Mike I don't know what to say. I don't know what I am feeling. All I know is that you ruined loads of my life and I can't really forgive you.'

Was that a good answer? He made me loose my leg, it was legitim to not give him another chance. Or did he deserve it? Well for once it was the truth and honestly, I did not understand what was going on in my body, in my mind actually. My brain controls my body so it's my brain that has feelings I cannot understand or creates feelings I cannot understand. He moved nearer. The chair made a screeching sound as its legs were dragged along the floor. He had to let go of my hand to complete this move. My hand felt empty, and I just wanted him to grab my hand again and just hold it. As soon as he had managed to place his stool beside mine, he put his one arm over my shoulder and held me in his arms. I started to rest my head on his shoulder, and he started to stroke my hair with his other hand. I felt so close to happy, if I knew what happiness was, it would be something close to this.

'Mike how is this going to end?' I asked.

'I have no idea, I just wish I could start over, but Mia I am the way I am and I just can't change it.'

'But what if we could change ourselves together, just imagine.'

'I am not worried about you. Mia. You can change as soon as I go, but there is no chance that I can change.'

'The only thing I can change is my existence, there is no point living the life I am living.'

Maybe I should not have said that. Now the person who would care knew, or might know, what I was up to.

'Unlike me Mia, you did nothing wrong. The bad things you have done are because of me, you can't blame yourself. I made you into the person you are today, you just need to forget your past and forget me.'

What the hell was he saying? Of course, he had brought me into these kinds of situations, but I was me because of me not because of him. It was not like I was his marionet. He could not control me like that. I was under no one's control, not even my own. So how the hell was he expecting me to be under his full control? I was not made by him. And there was no way I could forget everything, I just couldn't. That was not like me, that was the opposite of me. I needed to hold on to things, even the bad things. I could not forget, nor forgive.

Especially if he kept showing up in my life. I was lost inside my head and did not answer Mike's absurd statement. I was just there in his arms, like he had never done anything to me. Like he was an absolute angel no one needed to be afraid of. But maybe I should have been. Here in my apartment was the guy who ruined my life, the guy who had sent people to prison, the guy who had not only hurt people but also killed people, the guy who had done thousands of illegal things. The guy who had treated me like a slave, the guy who basically chopped of my leg. Despite all of that I was not afraid one tiny bit. On the contrary, I felt safe, I could not explain why. I know it did not make sense. It did not even make sense to me. Anyhow, I thought I should say something to him. But what? Should I ask him to leave? But I wanted him to stay. I just did not want him to say anything. I kinda wanted him to go, like, I felt safe but uncomfortable and at the same time I felt calm like it was a pleasant feeling having him near me. I could not make out my feelings.

'Mia I want to go and never meet you again. I think it will be the best for you. It's the only way for you to get back to normal life. I can't keep controlling you, it's not fair.'

But he was not controlling me. He just like made a few things happen in my life but no more. Maybe my life would have been shittier if I had not met Mike, maybe I would have died in a car crash or something. But would that have been so bad? I didn't know, and I probably never would. But that did annoy me. A lot. Everything happens for a reason though doesn't it?

'No, you can't do these things to me all these years and then just like leave me alone. That doesn't work.'

'It's the only way,' he said firmly.

There was no way to make this all good. But I guess I was the only one who got that, but anyway, was it even worth explaining? I don't think so. He would not understand, he would not even want to understand, in my opinion.

'But you can't do that to me. I don't want to be more alone than I already am, you took so much from me you can't just take yourself away from me too. Mike you can't leave me,' I cried out.

Maybe this was all part of his plan, maybe he wanted to see me suffer even more, maybe he still enjoyed seeing me suffer all the time. Maybe he had not changed, maybe he was just acting differently to mess me up. I did not understand him. He was a secret. And I was incapable of asking the things that I should, and that is why the mystery always grew bigger and turned more into misery. This might be the last time that I would see him and still no chance that I could bring myself to ask the questions I wanted to. He just stared into the wide-open room and said noting, I had a hard time to read his emotions.

The night went on and Mike never left. I liked thinking I did not let him leave but I'm not sure. He just stayed. My bed was so much better when I was not alone, my whole apartment was better. It was like someone had changed the filter covering my eyes. It was a completely different world almost. I nearly could not believe my eyes. Everything looked more cosy, more homely. But still, had I managed to be happy for a short period of time or was everything just imagination, like most things? Had it just been a dream again or was I living in reality, in the present? Just imagine, that would be amazing, being happy. I turned to look out the window which was in the wall beside my bed. The outside world looked soo much nicer. Usually, I would complain about the noisy cars, the smell of petrol, but today it seemed that a stream of fresh air was flowing in through the window, the outside was less grey, the colours were, like, brighter and there were rays of sunshine shining through the half-closed windows.

I turned over to Mike. I went to touch his cheek. But it was all cold. I had just left my hand there, thinking nothing. I moved closer to him, and I just felt something wet and sticky beside him. I felt a cold body alongside mine. Almost lifeless. His face was very pale, and his eyes had lost their shine. He did not react to anything. I could not feel his breath. I could not feel his heartbeat. I could not feel him. My heart started beating faster and my breaths got quicker. I put my hand to his heart again, then on his wrist then on his neck. But there was noting. Only his cold body was beside me. Lifeless Mike. I had imagined so many times for him to be gone, but I wanted him here. Here with me. But he was gone, like so many things in my life. He died or had killed himself, who knew? Well, he did, but he was gone. The tears started forming in my eyes and falling down my face. My hands were shaking, and my constant breathing did not help with the stress that I was in. Every part of me was in pain, I felt so out of place and every movement I made was uncomfortable. I was just so confused, yesterday had been good hadn't it? This must have been his plan all along. He always had a plan, no doubt. He wanted to do this to me. He wanted me to suffer, or I don't know what. I knew nothing at all. I had given away all my chances, I had messed up. It was time for me to leave this world, I was certain. I could die here right beside Mike, and we could leave this world together. There was really nothing anymore for me. I wanted to die. Now this second. I needed to go now. I could not bear this place anymore, could not bear myself anymore. I hated myself. I felt pain everywhere, even though nothing was touching me, except Mikes lifeless body. My tips of my fingers started to cramp up and the ache travelled all the way up to my head. I started to get a huge migraine and could not think anymore.

I hugged him so tightly, kissed his motionless lips and covered him in tears. I tried to talk to him, in the hope he would wake up. I tried pinching myself thinking I might just be in a bad dream. I wasn't. It was all real. I was feeling all these emotions, I was feeling something. I covered myself in waterworks. This time I would need to try something more radical, more dangerous. I looked back over to the window. The window was wide open and the blue and white striped curtains were pulled to the side. It was a welcome opening just waiting for me. I jumped up and ran to the window without looking back. And there I went. I jumped. It was the best feeling I had had in a long time, even better that being held in Mike's arms. I felt free inside I was just throwing the bad emotions from me, I was throwing away my anger, my fear, my helplessness, my guilt, my fear, my frustration away. One for one the horrid things were escaping into the sky, where they no more could be reached. Nothing mattered anymore. Everything was going to end. I would not need to endure any pain anymore. Everything was over. You cannot imagine my relief. I looked up to the sky and saw guise flying among my problems. The white clouds looked fluffier than they ever had. I turned my head back down and stared at the shinning black asphalt that covered the road. I noticed the trees and flowers that divided the pedestrian from the road. The trees were blooming, and the flowers were surrounded with tiny bumble bees I could barely see. The time had slowed down since I had jumped, I saw a screaming crowd, I saw heads turning. All the attention was directed towards me. I was the centre of attention. I mattered, my death would matter in these people's heads for the next few hours. I had noticed a small kid holding her stuffed bear pointing straight at me looking at her mom with concern. Before I could study her more, I felt my toe hit the ground. From there time started to move quicker. felt my bones crumbling as I hit the ground, I could hear the sound of them breaking. I could feel them shattering, but no pain just relief. I had no potential in this world. I had done the right thing. While I was falling through the air, I felt no regret, it felt like the best decision in my life. I loved how I had not questioned my own death anymore and had just let it happen. The last thing I saw were people running towards me, concerned and shocked in all their humanity. Women screaming. These people were peasants, they had a happy life and wanted others not to end theirs, but I just had.

Was I dead? I think I was. I did not see anything. I did not hear anything. Just me in my own head. Did this happen to all people who died? This state probably would end soon too. Was I finally gone? The only thing left, my soul. The last things that went through my mind were the moments I had cherished in my life. My childhood memories rushed through my mind like a movie, I thought about the times we had camped in the wide woods, I remembered my science fair awards, my childhood friends. I felt the accomplishment again I had felt in high school after graduating and getting a scholarship. I felt the love and care from my parents that had gone missing over the years. I had pictured my first kiss. I recalled the good times at the factory and the times I had laughed and danced. My muscles were not working anymore, nevertheless I felt myself smile. I My mind was filled with happiness, I was content. And then everything went black, I could no more paint out pictures in my head and the voice in my mind started to fade.

HAPPINESS IS ONLY A PHASE

I could already smell the coffee my husband was making for me. I was so lucky to be married to someone like him. He would do everything for me, just like I would do for him. We were perfect together. I got out of my fluffy sheets that I loved so dearly. I slipped into my soft slippers and followed the scent of coffee down the stairs that were covered in carpet. With every step I would sink in a bit and leave a trail. If you looked at the stairs a few seconds after you could see where I had walked. It was Monday, which meant that I would be working the late shift. I loved my job as much I loved my free time. I walked down the stairs and peered out the window. The sun was shining outside and the blooming trees in front of our apartment were swaying in the wind. What a beautiful day.

'Good morning, dear, did you sleep well?' he asked.

'Very, you?' I asked back.

'Also, here's your coffee, just as you like it.'

'Thank you.' How was I such a lucky girl?, I asked myself.

I took a small sip of the still hot, delicious coffee. This was the best way to start the day. He put a plate with a slice of toast, a fried egg and some strawberries in front of me. I enjoyed it thoroughly and then before I was done brushing my teeth he called, 'Bye! Have an amazing day, amazing woman.'

'Bye,' I replied.

I finished up in the kitchen, grabbed my lunch, which my husband had put on the table, and hurried down to my car. I did not want to be late. I preferred to arrive a bit earlier.

I drove the short thirty minutes to the hospital where I worked as a nurse. I loved my job. Caring for people just gave me pleasure, I guess. There were of course downsides and tragedies but overall, it was positive. Like always I was warmly greeted by everyone. I worked in the intensive care station. At the moment, there was a young boy who had been in an awful car crash, but he was getting better. I went in his room, changed his sheets, checked all his vitals, and refilled his feeding tube. I went from room to room doing the same, making notes for the doctors, refilling and replacing, changing sheets, just checking on the patients. There was a new woman in today. I entered her room and the first thing I had to do is hold my hand over my mouth. Her appearance scared me. I felt so bad for her. How could this have happened? She was scarred all over her body. Apparently, she had fallen from a window. But she had been lucky because she did not damage her spine at all. The damage was vast, she could have been paralyzed. Thankfully she was not, just scarring all over, two broken legs, a broken arm, some internal bleeding, and a concussion. She had had major surgery yesterday when she was brought to the hospital because of the internal bleeding, but she got through the surgery well. At the moment she was sleeping, under anaesthesia, but I was sure she would wake up soon. As soon as her body had a bit of energy, everything was going to be fine.

By lunch I had gone through all the patients' rooms and now I was enjoying the salmon, rice, and beans that my husband had made me. It was such lovely weather I sat with my colleagues around a table outside, just chatting. If one of the patients woke up from their coma it was my job to talk to them, make sure they were ok. Sometimes patients were confused when they woke up and I was there to explain to them what had happened and later to explain the same things to their families, friends, and relatives. Basically, whoever came to visit them or pick them up. I also would need to figure out if they had any damages or disabilities due to the coma. But this only occurred rarely, mostly the patients came around eventually. I just loved my job.

After I had finished my lunch, I made my way back into the hospital. In the afternoon I took blood from three of my patients and brought it to the lab in order for it to be analysed. I also did more checks on patients, and I was allowed to let one patient go home. His parents had been thrilled to take him home. I think he was happy about the fact too. Well, of course who would not be? He had been in the hospital for two months, after he had been violently attacked on the street. The stories that brought people here were really just like out of the movies. Before I had worked here, I never imagined things like this happening so often.

I got in my car and drove off. On my way home I got a phone call from my husband, Brice.

'Hey, how was your day?' he asked.

'Great, you?'

'Long, but I am done now and hearing your voice makes the whole day so much better. You make my day everyday.'

'You're such a charmer.'

'Would you like Chinese takeout for dinner? I'll be home in about an hour. I could pick it up on the way if you like.'

'Spring rolls and vegetable noodles, please.'

'Got it.'

'Thank you dear.'

'You're welcome, see you at home.'

'Byee.'

'Byee, be careful on the road.'

'Of course, bye now.'

I hung up and concentrated on the road in front of me. I hated driving a car. It was so boring and I was always afraid of having an accident. I had seen enough of what happens to people who get into car crashes. I really did not want that. It scared me, the thought that on any given day there was a chance of having a severe accident. It could happen anytime, anywhere. The thought scared me; I would never want to give up what I have. My life was everything. I could not imagine losing everything. I tried to concentrate on the road again. Eventually I was singing along to the songs in the radio even though I was a terrible singer. I was enjoying myself. I was looking forward to the sticky noodles and crunchy spring rolls I was going to eat as soon as I came home. My mouth was watering just thinking about it. I could almost taste the noodles, smell the ginger, the soy sauce. This was going to be great. I parked my car and went up to my apartment. I set the table and turned on the television to watch the news while I finished clearing up the dishes from the morning. I knew Brice had arrived when I heard someone honk multiple times. I went out to the balcony to see him carrying two big plastic bags out of his car. I went down to help him. As soon as he saw me he dropped both bags on the floor and hugged me and kissed me on the neck. His hands help me firmly around my waist.

'You don't need to strip me here,' I said.

'I could though,' he replied.

'The Chinese is getting cold.'

'So, food is more important than me.'

He made a sad face and I kissed him on the lips as soft as I could, then grabbed the Chinese and ran up the stairs.

'Maybe,' I called.

He came after me at a normal speed. Before he could even take of his shoes and jacket, I had bitten into the first spring roll. He gave me a look and then laughed. It tasted soo good.

'I just can't take you seriously ', he said.

With spring roll in my mouth I answered, 'To bad.'

We both sat down and enjoyed our meal. I had turned off the television because the two of us enjoyed talking over dinner. We told each other about our days at work as usual. He worked as a banker in a bank, well obviously, about fifty miles from our house. But he did not like his job as much as I did. It was a bit boring, I guess. After, we cleaned up the kitchen, which took forever even though it was only take out. We would always joke and tease each other in a playful way, like we had just fallen in love. We decided that we were going to watch a movie before bed, the both of us did not like going to bed too early. We liked getting enough sleep but if we went to bed too early we would just end up bugging each other and never sleeping. We were really like fifteen-year-olds. I felt nowhere near thirty-two, even though I had a job, a husband and an apartment. Ok, I did not have any kids, but I had never been sure if I wanted any. Cause I knew both me and Brice would not want to give up our careers and no way did I want to have kids that were only in day care centres and taken care by nannies and babysitters. I did not want that for my child or my children.

Halfway through the move, Brice left me alone because one of his old mates had called him. He had gone out on the balcony to talk to him so I could not make out what they were talking about. It seemed so secretive. But I trusted him. Surely, they were talking about old times, maybe the things he had done were embarrassing. I was a little annoyed that I could not overhear their conversation, but I knew that it was nothing bad, so I continued watching the movie. However, their call was going on for quite long, a lot longer than usual and that was starting to stress me out. I just started wondering again. What could they be talking about? I did not dare to go close enough so I could hear. turned my body and watched my husbands body language. He did not seem happy, he seemed to be sad or maybe angry. He was walking in circles and pausing in random places staring at his feet. I am sure it was nothing bad I was just worrying about noting. I pressed play on the movie again. I enjoyed watching movies to calm down at night but like I wish that they would be more interesting because before the movie was even half done, I would already know how it would end, but even so I had to finish watching it. The phone call had been going on for quite some time cause the movie had ended, exactly the way I had expected. I was drinking a green tee when Brice opened the porch door. It always made a screeching sound. He came and sat down across from me.

'How was the movie honey?' he asked.

'Good, what were you talking about?'

'Oh don't worry, nothing important. Just about old times and how we are all doing.'

'Ok. I think I am going to go to bed.'

He stood up and came over to me kissed me on the forehead and went to the counter to make himself a tea. His eyes were slightly red and it looked like he had been crying. But he never cried. It must of just been his hay fever. I went upstairs and got ready for bed. It was always quite the occasion cause I would shower, brush my teeth, put my hair up, meditate and stretch and then lay down and awake for quite a bit of time. I had always had trouble falling asleep, but eventually I did. I had not even noticed Brice coming up. What had he been doing this whole time. I tried to ignore it but it left me restless. From downstairs I heard a faint voice, was he on the phone again. I tried to listen to overhear the conversation. But I couldn't. I felt bad invading his privacy.

I woke up the next morning not really restored. It was Tuesday, which meant that Brice was out on an early run. I got up and prepared our breakfast and lunch. Before I went, I left Brice a little note, like I always did. Just telling him I love him and that he should not forget his lunch. And so, I was off again to work. I did the usual check-up on the patients.

When I went to check on the patient who had fallen three storeys, she had woken up. I think she was utterly confused, cause she continuously had asked me where she was and if this was heaven. She seemed very lost. But who would not be? It must be such a weird feeling waking up from an induced coma. She had been under anaesthesia the other day but apparently, she had to be rushed into another surgery because she had problems with her heart which would have led to heart failure, so they had to induce a coma. Normally, she would not wake up till she had pulled enough strength together. But occasionally it happened that patients woke up for short period of time. This, I guess, had been the case, cause after two minutes of asking questions she fell back asleep, well asleep if you can call it that.

I had always wondered how it must feel to be in a coma and to wake up from it. I knew some patients did not recall anything from when they were in a coma, but some remembered something – like that someone had said something or that they had been touched – but always very faded memories. The day went on and nothing more special happened. Brice came to pick me up at the hospital cause I had lent my car to my colleague for the weekend. Hers had broken down and she had to go and see her grandmother miles away from here. We had two cars, so I was happy to lend it to her. I knew she was grateful, and I loved seeing people happy and whatever I would give would come back to me one day in some way or another. When I put my hand on the cool metal of the car door to get inside, I already saw in his face that something was wrong. He looked off and when I got in, he did not greet me as he usually did but just sat there in silence. When I looked in his eyes his just turned away. Maybe he had just had a bad day at work.

'What's up dear?' I asked.

'Nothing.'

'You can tell me.'

He said nothing and stepped on the gas pedal. He did not turn to me while he talked he was just looking straight ahead. I felt like I was being ignored.

'We're over the speed limit.'

I think he was able to pull himself together and slow down. But he said nothing and just looked at me. I was not able to make out anything from the expression on his face. I had never seen a look like this on his face in the eight years I had known him. I just turned my head hoped that he would say something, and everything would make sense, but he never did. At that moment I felt uncomfortable looking at him. I did not like seeing him like this and I did not want to let him know that I was worried. I tried focusing, I tried counting the houses that we passed to distract me. But nothing worked. I was getting worried, I might just be getting worried over nothing once again, but what if I wasn't, what if there was something. He turned into our driveway. I just sat there still staring outside. I could see our balcony. He had been out there for quite some time yesterday.

'Are you coming?' he called.

I stood up, opened the door and followed him upstairs. What had happened to the soo bubbly person I thought I knew so well; that I trusted so deeply. Did he trust me as much I trusted him?

I walked up the stairs and did not even lift my head once. I just followed the steps with my eyes, watching my feet go in front of each other. He held the door open for me and I entered our apartment.

He was different, he was acting off. I put down my stuff and went to the kitchen. I needed to distract myself. I pulled open the fridge and felt the coolness hit my face. I pulled out multiple stuff to cook some pasta. Usually, he would be right here beside me, bugging me, helping me. But he was far away, lying on the sofa like he was in a coma. Just like my patients. I was getting kind of mad at this situation. I had lived with him for five years and he had never acted like this. I started almost throwing the pasta into the water that I had started boiling a few minutes before. I had almost lost the cardboard package in the water. I cut tomatoes furiously, I was surprised I did not cut off my own fingers. Luckily I only chopped the air or the tomatoes. I started tossing it all in a pan to create something near a sauce. Every few seconds I would look over to the living room to see if Brice would say something, do something, give me a familiar expression. But nothing. I just wanted to know what was up. I wanted to help.

'Ouch, shit!'

Shit! I just had poured water over my hands, my mind was definitely not where it was supposed to be. I started shaking my hands in the air in order to reduce the pain. I was quite unsuccessful. I poured a shit load of cold water over my hands to stop the burn hurting too much.

'Don't swear like that', he exclaimed. He had not even looked over to see if everything was ok and he had never told me off for swearing. Something was not right. I wanted to know what it was, I wanted to know if it was me. Was I being a bad wife or a bad person? Or was he getting bored of me? I just wanted to know.

'Dinner is ready,' I told him in a low voice.

He stood up very slowly from the sofa where he had been lying in silence. He sat down, the chair made a sound cause he had sat down so hard, with soo much force like his legs had just collapsed. I served him my pasta and questionable sauce. I put the salad on the table and got the cheese that I had forgotten out of the fridge. He just started eating slowly, twirling his pasta around his fork till almost the whole plateful was wound around his fork. He tried to put it in his mouth but then realized he had way too much. He put it back down and started over again, twirling his fork. Then he grabbed the packet of cheese and sprinkled a whole lot over everything. He was eating but without the usual joy.

'Please, please tell me what is up! You can't pretend it's nothing. I know you; something is up. I am begging you, tell me. I can't bare seeing you like this.'

'Nothing,' he yelled, with food still in his mouth. He did not look up. I felt like he did not want to meet eyes with me.

Why was he getting mad? What had I done to upset him so deeply? I could just not imagine what had happened.

'I am sure it's not nothing. You know that you can tell me any and everything. I have always been here for you, and I always be. Please just tell me even if it something small.'

'You're such a typical woman, always wanting to know everything, never letting a man be.'

He had never talked like this to me, like he was discriminating against women. I took my plate and left the kitchen. I sat down in our bed, pulled the covers over me and ate my pasta in bed. I felt the tears coming. I felt my heart go cold and shivers pass through my body. I did not feel like eating anymore. I put the pasta down on the floor, covered myself with the blanket and just tried get rid of this awful feeling in every centimeter of my body.

PHASE 2 DESTRUCTION

Our relationship got worse and worse with every day that passed. We did not talk and if we did it was more like an argument. I just tried to ignore the fact of what was going on and concentrate on my work. I was hoping that soon he would just come up to me and apologize, explain all of it and everything would be fine again and we could go back to what we were before all of this.

A couple of days later he had not even come up to sleep in our bed but had dragged a pillow and a blanket downstairs to the living room. I was fed up fighting and just accepted that he was not going to change his tune. I kept thinking that I was the problem, what had I done? I missed the old him. I missed the smallest things like smelling the coffee that he made in the morning before I made my way to work. I had thought of it as I sipped my fresh coffee this morning. He made better coffee. I had not made coffee in such a long time – he had always made it for me. He had treated me like a princess and now he was treating me like I didn't exist. I thought about calling my sister. I knew that I could trust her and talk about it to her. However, I did not want to bother her. She had a lot going on with her kids and husband and was always busy. I did not just want to wast her time for my problems.

I went to the hospital again. I checked up on all the patients. The one patient, Mia, had woken up yesterday and Grace, my co-worker, filled me in with what had happened when she had woken up during her night shift.

'You won't believe it Ava, she woke up and would not stop screaming and asking questions. I have never seen a patient like this. It seems like she has really gone crazy. She was out of her mind. I think she asked me at least five times if she had landed in heaven or hell. Then she started mumbling stuff to herself. Honestly, I felt sorry for her, she looked like she was hurt-

110

ing herself just by thinking, you know what I mean. It's hard to explain, but it is how it felt.'

'This really sounds odd. Maybe she is just confused from the coma. It must be a weird feeling waking up from it.'

'Could be. Well good luck on our shift. I will be on my way home.'

'Have a nice day, bye,' I called after her as she was leaving the staff room.

Now I was kinda excited to go and check up on Mia. I thought this would give me a bit of life. I was sure it was going to be hard, but I loved a challenge, and I was ready to take this one. I went to her room first. Even though my checks did not usually start there I could not wait. I was unsure if I was allowed to be excited about a patient that was different than the others. I wondered if things like this gave me rushes of adrenaline. I entered the room. She sat there, upright with her head leaning against the wall, her eyes all on me.

'Thank God, someone else. Please tell me that I am in heaven. Please,' she pleaded.

I went over to her and sat down on the edge of her bed.

'Look, you were just in a coma and are in the hospital. You might be a bit confused at the moment but don't worry, me and all my co-workers will be here to guide you through these difficult times and get you all the help that you need.'

'Am I not dead?,' she asked.

'No you are as alive as you can be. Let me check your blood pressure, would you?', I asked.

'What? I am dead. I know it.'

'Look, you see this monitor, this is your heartrate and the rest of your vital signs. You're alive.'

She started swearing and hitting the empty air with her still weak arms. I tried to grab them to bring her to a stop and calm her down, but I was not so successful. Eventually she calmed down and I managed to catch hold of her arms. I heard her breathing heavily, even a few sweat drops were forming on her forehead. Her heartrate had gone up quite a bit.

'It's all ok, you're going to be fine. You just need to calm down a bit.'

'Nothing is fine if I am still alive,' she hollered.

'Trust me, life is such a precious gift and you were so lucky to get it,' I reasoned with her. It seemed like she was not listening. Like she was so certain that she was right.

She said nothing more. I checked her vitals and made some notes and went back to check up on the other patients. I wondered what was wrong with this lady. She had said nothing was fine if she was still alive. Was she depressed or even suicidal? I would have to remember to look in her report and maybe make a few little notes just to be sure.

All the other patients were doing fine in comparison to her, at least mentally. The few words that had come out of her mouth had only been negative. I think I would need to get a counsellor or someone to help her. I was not sure if I could.

I was on my way home and realized that I had forgotten about everything that was happening in my own home. But now it was coming at me like waves. I was going to confront him today no matter how big the argument. I was going to scream my lungs out till he told me what was up. I had the right to know. I was his wife. I slammed the door of the car when I had parked and marched up the stairs full of confidence. I felt angry, not necessarily at him but at the situation. I put my hand on the doorknob, took a deep breath and closed my eyes briefly and went in. I put my stuff down and holding my head up I walked over to him, sat down beside him on the coach, grabbed his hands and waited for his attention. It took a lot longer than normal.

'I need to know what is going on. You've got to tell me. I can't go on like this. Please.'

He looked at me, seemingly baffled by this confidence that had been lacking the last few days. I felt the tears start forming in my eyes. I tried to hold them back but there was no way, they were coming too fast. I could not describe the emotions I was having. I felt his heartbeat get faster. His palms stared to get moist. He looked at me like if I was going to say if you don't want to you don't have to. But their was no choice here, he had to.

'I am sorry, I know you are worried, and I hate it when you get worried, but I can't tell you I just can't. Don't worry, it's really nothing. It will be over soon and you can get on with your life.

'Just tell me. I don't care what it is. I just need to know. I don't want to get on with my life, I want to get on with our life Don't you understand?'

Did he not understand how much pain he was causing me like this.

'I can't I am sorry, its nothing.'

It was certainly not nothing, the way he was acting and slowly I was losing my initial confidence.

'It's not nothing. Tell me, now,' I screamed.

I had lost my patience too and the longer he did not answer the crosser I got at him. I had always thought of myself as a calm and patient person, but I was proving myself wrong. He said nothing, stood up grabbed a beer out of the fridge and left the apartment, slamming the door as he went. I got up and ran after him.

I had wanted to curse at him but had stopped myself at our front door. Holding my breath and trying to calm down. I heard his car roaring of. I knew that meant nothing good. I lay down on the sofa, putting my head on a pillow. I felt my body trembling with fear. I was scared. What was he going to do? Not to me but to himself. When he got wasted and had no one to watch over him he did the most stupid things. I got so cold that I covered myself with all the blankets that I could find. I huddled myself into a ball and just cried till my eyes were dry. One of the blankets was the one he had been using to sleep on the sofa and I could smell him like he was there with me, but he was not; he was somewhere else, probably drinking, doing stupid things he might regret. I was getting so afraid that I got my sad self to get up and go down to the car to drive into town to look for him. I know that that would be that last thing he wanted me to do but I did not care if he got mad at me. In any case, at that moment I was afraid for his safety.

I drove all over town, probably looking totally weird with my red face and still in my working clothes. I did not care though, I just wanted to find my beloved husband. I checked every bar, but no one had seen him, and if I saw people, I knew they would be concerned about me and not him. 'You are looking so terrible Ava, what's wrong? Come have a drink with us and talk.' But I did not want to. I carried on and after a four-hour search, I gave up in the hope. He would come home eventually, wouldn't he?

I almost fell asleep driving home. Now even my own safety was at risk. As I opened the front door, I was hoping that I would just see him there asleep drunk on the sofa, but our apartment was lifeless, no one was there. I went back to the spot on the couch I had been before and just tried to imagine him being here by smelling the sheets. Eventually I fell asleep. When I woke up it was no more morning but more like lunchtime. I could tell because the sun was shining so bright in through the windows. It came from a different angle in the morning. I was off work today, usually I would be back from a run or a walk with my husband. Just the thought of it made me whimper. I slowly made my way over to the kitchen, grabbed a box of cereal off the shelf and poured milk and sugar over it. Screw healthy eating. I sat down and just barely managed to bring the spoon with cereal to my mouth without shaking so much that it didn't fall on the floor or the table. The cereal tasted disgusting. I sat there just waiting for a miracle or something.

I started looking at the photos hung up on the fridge. There was one of us together at the Niagara Falls, one of us after the Honolulu marathon, one of us here and there. Only us. What was I without him? Nothing. My family would maybe disown me out of shame. I went over to the living room and sat down on the floor looking through photo albums. I knew it was going to make everything more painful, but I wanted vivid memories of him. I wanted to remember every little detail. I heard the phone ring, I sprung up and hurried over. I hoped it was him. Or at least some news. I needed him more badly than I ever.

'Hello, Ava speaking,' I answered.

'Hello, is this Ms Collins?'

'Yes,' I said, almost intimidated.

'We are calling from the NYU Medical Centre. Your husband Brice was admitted last night, after he got into a car accident. We need you to come here as soon as possible. Don't worry, he is fine.'

I hung up without even answering, grabbed everything and ran to the car. I drove to the hospital constantly over the speed limit. Ticket or not, I needed to get there. What had happened? Was he driving drunk? Did he hurt anyone? Had he hurt himself? Had they needed to pump out his stomach from all the alcohol? Had he suffered a heart attack? Was he attacked on the streets by some gang and been robbed? I know I was making up stories inside my head but what else should I have done? I ran into the hospital with my car parked badly and not locked. Looking like I had just gotten out of a hurricane.

'I ... em, I am here for Brice Collins, I am here to see my husband.' I tried to get the words out of my mouth, but I was gasping for air.

I had never run that fast in my life. The nurse at the reception told me to follow her. I wished she would walk faster and bring me to Brice. She opened the door for me and he was there, eyes closed, in hospital clothes, covered by white linen, in a bed. To other people he might have looked ill and weak but to me he looked handsome, great. I had missed him so much, even though I had seen him a few hours before. I went over and lay down beside him, hugged him, wating for him to respond but he did not even open his eyes and look at me. My eyes stared to become watery, and tears started to flow. The nurse sat down in the corner of the room, probably to give me some space and time. I grabbed Brice's hand, and they weren't warm like they usually were, but cold, lacking something, I don't know what. But I could feel that he knew I was there and that filled my heart, and made me a bit less scared.

'Don't worry your husband will be awake in a bit. He is just recovering from the meds we gave him last night to calm him down when we pumped his stomach out. He had been drinking a lot. He was lucky nothing happened to him when he crashed into the lamp post. Do you know if he has ever had any alcohol problems before?,' she asked.

'No he has never been addicted, but I know that something has been off lately.'

He just drank in that way when something was terribly wrong. I had only seen him drink a lot on two other occasions.

'Well, I will leave you for a bit,' she said calmly.

'Thank you,' I said. I knew how hard such situations were to manage. I was just one other obnoxious wife.

What was I going to do with my man? He was not an alcoholic, was he? Was that what he had been keeping from me? Even if he was, I would still love him and more than anything I would want to help him. I just lay there beside my still and silent husband, feeling like I was living through a midlife crisis. But I was not sure how things would be when he woke up. They could get worse.

'Ava is that you?' he asked.

I felt his one hand touch my shoulder. I had fallen into a light sleep beside him. I turned to him and kissed him all over the face.

'I love you.'

'Love you too.'

'How are you feeling?' I asked.

'Fine, but do you think you could find me something to eat? I am starving.'

I leaped to my foot and went to the small cafe right beside the reception and grabbed him a croissant and an orange juice. I came back into his room and standing beside his bed there was a doctor and the nurse from before. They saw me, their voices went down in volume, I could hear the doctor say that he need not be afraid and there was no sense in doing things like that and that everything was going to be fine. What were they talking about? what was the thing I did not know? I went over to his bed and set the bottle and the paper bag on the night table.

'Thank you dear,' he said.

The doctor reached for my hand.

'Nice to meet you Miss Collins. I am Dr. Hendrick, but please call me William,' he said.

'Nice to meet you to,' I replied.

I sat back down on the side of the bed.

'I think your husband has something to tell you.'

I thought so too, and now there was no way out for him. But as excited I was, I was also anxious. I felt the fear creeping up inside of me.

'Can I talk to her on my own?'

'Of course,' William answered.

Was this a good or a bad sign?

'Ava, please don't freak out. I think you know that I have been keeping something from you, but it was only to protect you cause I know you all too well and I know how you react to certain things.'

'But you know that you can tell me everything. '

I just wished he would tell me. The more I waited, the more stories I made up in my mind.

'I know but sometimes telling everything does not end well. But I guess I am left with no other choice. And telling it makes it truer and its harder to ignore the fact. Just don't be mad I did not tell you. I have been diagnosed with colorectal cancer.'

I saw his eyes getting all teared up. My tears were already coming. Why had he not told me? This could not be happening! Everything seemed totally surreal. This could not be happening. Not to me. Not to him. It was not fair. What had we done to deserve this?

'Which stage?' I asked anxiously.

'Stage four.' There was a pause. 'Look I don't know if I will survive all the treatments and all the chemo, and I am sorry for not telling you. I know I should have but I could not bring myself to it. I was terrified I still am.'

I went as close as I could to him and wrapped him in a hug and just cried all over him. 'You're not allowed to die.'

'I won't, and you're ok on your own anyway. Just promise me one thing now.'

'What?'

'That you will always remember me, but keep on living. And that you will be the person I fell in love with, the person who always helps everyone, who is always friendly and makes so many people smile.'

'That is more than one thing.'

We both chuckled. I saw a small smile through his wall of tears and fear.

'See, you even make me laugh in a place and situation like this. I love you,' he said.

'You will never love me like I love you.'

Dr. Hendrick came back in and looked over at us. I saw in his face that he knew what had been going on.

'Miss Collins, I see the right thing has happened. Please don't take it hard. It's a tough situation to be in, you need to understand that.'

I just shook my head in response. You know when you shake your head so hard that you feel a bit sick. Well, that was the case.

'Miss Collins, in about a half an hour I will have to take your husband for an appointment, I think it would be best if you would go home get cleaned up and rest. I know you might need a bit of time to process all of this.'

I nodded again. But I did not want to leave. I just wanted to freeze myself in this moment.

'But ...'

'You can ask all the questions you want to the nurse that you have already met. She will be at the front desk. Her name is Isabella. She will be happy to help you.'

After that he left I just lay there beside my husband trying to absorb him. That sounded not quite right but that is how it felt. The nurse Isabella came in and asked me to follow her. After a bit of pleading for a few more minutes I got up. I knew myself all too well how annoying people were that acted like me in the hospital.

'Don't worry Miss Collins, we will do our best to help your husband get healthy again.'

'How long has he been diagnosed with cancer?' I asked.

'Not too long ago. He came here about a week ago because he was concerned about things that were happening to him. He told us that he had felt extremely tired lately and that his stool had blood in it. We ran a few tests and three days later we figured out that he had colorectal cancer that had already spread quite far. He was supposed to come to the hospital immediately so we could start with the treatment, but he must have been scared and of course no one wants to just come to the hospital. When he was brought in here last night through a coincidence, I saw him and I told the doctor that had pumped out his stomach. So maybe it was luck that he got into all of that.'

I could not listen to this anymore. I just wanted to drown myself in hot chocolate and hide myself under my covers. And think that all the problems would be gone when I woke up.

'Thank you for everything. Have a nice day ', I said with the closest thing to a smile I could manage.

I got in my car and sobbed the whole way home, hoping for some light at the end of the tunnel. Maybe just maybe it had been good that I had made him mad yesterday because otherwise he would have not gone out to drink, and he would not have ended up in in the hospital and God knows what would have happened then? However, alcohol was probably not the best thing in his situation. I did not know how I should feel. I was relived to finally know what was up but knowing it did not really make me feel better. I was driving super slow cause there was no way that I could concentrate on the road while I was thinking like this. I did not do anything the whole weekend I only went to the hospital a second time to visit Brice, but it did not make me feel good. He was so weak he barley spoke, barely moved. He just lay there and looked at me and I would cry and cry. If he spoke, he would say stop crying dear or I love you or I feel tired but that was about it. I heard my alarm ring, and I did not spring out of bed like I usually did. I did not have my usual motivation for the day, how should I? But I somehow managed to get out of bed, drink a coffee and get to the hospital where I worked. Why did

I work in this hospital and not in the other one where my husband was? Well, there was a fair number hospitals and medical centres in New York. Why did this stupid place have separate hospitals? I did my usual at work but differently. Every movement that I did was slow and not routine. Everything needed so much thinking in order for it not to go wrong. I went through the patients, checking on them everything was normal till I came upon the one woman who had already messed a bit with my head. I came in, it had seemed like she was asleep but with her eyes open, like she was in her own world. She would not take her eyes off me. She watched my every action.

'Can you like just unplug me?' she asked, so out of the blue that I got startled.

'Sorry what did you say?' I was unsure of what I had just heard.

I wondered if I had just misunderstood. It took me a while to realize what she wanted. I did not even know if I had heard right, or if I had imagined it.

'There are tubes all all over a and I know I if you ju just took the the one out for fo od and waaater you could just ttt let me star ve here or de hydrate. Then every thi thing would be ooo-ver. Plllllease, I am begiiing youuuu. I s see n noo other way. I can't stay here. Its tort torture. Please.'

It had taken her forever to form her words. They were coming out slowly and I had to really concentrate to catch what she was saying. She could barely move her mouth, it seemed that she was putting all her energy in forming these sentences for me. I was shocked. and I did not know what I should say or do. I was overwhelmed. I was more overwhelmed than I had already been with my own situation. I did not know what to do. If she only knew how broken my own life was. I sat down on the chair that was beside her bed.

'I can't, I could never. It would be illegal, and I would have such a bad conscience I could never get rid of it. And I am sure you would regret it too. You will feel so much better as soon as you can get back to your normal life. Just imagine seeing your family again, your friends, your partner or husband if you have one. Just imagine all the great memories that you will create in the future, just imagine how full your life will be after this rough patch in your life,' I tried to explain to her.

I was talking so much positive shit to her, but I was the opposite of positive myself. But really, I was trapped in my fear. My fear of losing the person I loved most, who loved me.

'Pleas eee, you don't kn know how grate ful I would b be. There is not thing here he for me.'

I needed to get her a psychologist. It would help her, and I would inform her family that she was here. I was not sure what she had told them and I was sure that she was not going to tell me.

'Look this is not my area of expertise, but I think that you will get better and I will do everything in my power to help you. I will get a psychiatrist down here for you. I am sure their team would be able to help you.'

'No wa way, anything other than a psych viat rist. I can't handlve any more more of anted peo ple. Look lady, I know yo u are try trying to do yyu ur job, but for ggget your job and try to be in my sit uation. Plea ssse let the torturr re end. I jummm ped out of that win dow to kill my ssself and I did not even manage to do it. I don't want to be hereee, just like let me lea ve this world. And no more psych iat rists,' she said.

What did that mean no more psychiatrists? I understood her so well, maybe I was feeling the same way at the moment, but I would never want to kill myself. Just imagine the sadness and grief I would bring upon the people that I know. But I thought I would wait with getting her a psychiatrist, I think she really did not want that and I did not want to push her too much. She was in a way too fragile state.

'I will get you some chocolate or something to cheer you up.'

I went to my bag and got out a chocolate that I had taken with to cheer me up a bit, but I wanted to help her and that would cheer me up. I went back to her room and gave her the chocolate and I think she tried to give me something that was close to a smile. Like thank you no thank you. I left and continued my work. I promised myself that I would go visit her after my shift to see how she was doing. Once again, I was seeing happy faces take their daughter, son, or whatever home. I had a small glimpse of bliss, but then I was constantly thinking how my husband must be doing. I knew too much about what could happen to people with colorectal cancer. I knew all too well that it ran in his family, that his grandfather had passed away due to it. I could remember that not every treatment was successful, and I was afraid cause I knew how bad his already was. He probably had just refused to acknowledge that something was wrong for a long time. Probably, he was just as scared as me. I packed up my handbag and was almost regretting giving her the chocolate bar this morning. I could have used that right now. But she had needed it more, no? I went over to her room and pushed open the heavy door. She was sleeping under the light blue sheets or at least I thought she was. She opened her eyes slowly after the door had closed and made a very unbearable sound.

'Are you awake Miss David?'

'Of course I am. There is no way that I could sleep in my condition. What, are you actually thinking I am happy if I can just shut my eyes for a bit?'

One good sign was that she was speaking more clearly now. She was improving. She was going to be a fast recoverer.

'How are you feeling?' I asked.

'I feel like making you unplug me and letting me die right here in this bed.'

'You know I won't do that,' I said.

I tried to keep my head down. I did not want to meet her eyes, which were filled with desperation and agony.

'What do I know?' she exclaimed.

'I am pretty sure you know that there are people out there that cherish you and want you to get through this,' I said.

'I am sure there are not.'

'What about your family?' I asked.

'They don't care.'

'Your friends?'

'Non-existent.'

'Look I don't know a lot about you but I know that I want you to make it. Every person has a purpose, you just need to find it. Every life is valuable, and I know how it is losing someone, trust me.'

' Ya, but my life does not matter. I don't even feel human anymore. There is no point. Please just help me end everything.'

'I can't. I could never live with the thought. My mind is a big mess anyway already.'

'You're telling me that! My mind is such a mess that I want to die.'

'It's probably just a phase you need to live through.'

'You don't understand. Look, you've probably got a perfect life with good relationships. When you leave me you probably going to go home to your husband or boyfriend, girlfriend partner or something. Unlike me you have a life. You have things that you enjoy. You have happiness.'

'Shut up, no one's life is perfect. No one's life is perfect. My husband has fucking cancer and I am fucking scared, so that is definitely far from perfect,' I said loudly.

It was so unprofessional to talk to a patient like that. I was shocked by my own action and held my hand over my mouth. But it had just come out of my mouth without any thought behind it. I did not regret it. However, it was wrong.

'I am sorry. But what I am saying is that mine is so horrible that I cannot deal with it anymore. It is too much for me to handle so just let me be. You would not understand anyway.'

'I know that I might not understand but I would at least see you a bit better if you would talk about it, then I could at least try to understand.'

'I don't want to talk about it, I just wanna die now.'

'Please don't say things like that.'

'I will say whatever I want lady. You don't need to tell me what I am allowed to do and what not. No one can do that.'

'I won't. I am just trying to give you some advice here that could help you, cause that is all I want. I want to help you.'

'Sure, that is what everyone wants, but it's your job, you do it for a living. What's the point? You're just another nurse, another worker in the health care system. You are all the same anyway.'

That struck me. How could this lady tell me something like that? I was not just a nurse; I loved my job, I tried my best all the time, I generally cared about the wellbeing of my patients. To me it was not just my job. I tried to stay calm, I took a few breaths in and paused before I continued.

'Of course it is my job, but I love my job and I think it is more than my job. It is my passion, it gives me meaning in my life.'

'Sure, I thought my job was a way of pursuing my passion once but it is bullshit. There is no such thing as passion. It is just another emotion us humans have invented. We just let ourselves think that we are passionate about something to prevent everyone killing themselves. There is no point in doing a job cause there is no happiness involved, no point.'

I had a hard time making sense of everything she said.

'I am sure you would find joy and purpose in a job again. You just need to find the right one. Can I ask you what your job used to be?', I asked shyly.

'I used to work for a large pharmaceutical company.'

'So, you had a pretty good job. Why were you not happy with it?'

'I know that I was in a good position. Money was not a problem, but I somehow had lost the initial motivation that I had begun with, and I saw no point. I was getting nowhere. I knew that I should be happy with my job, so I tried to force myself to be happy. I was constantly searching for the feeling I knew I had to feel.'

'What do you mean?'

'I was developing a drug to treat cancer, but I got nowhere, and I didn't even see a point in developing it cause there is no point in life. So, what is the point of healing patients with cancer? It's not worth it. I thought making this drug was my passion, but it was not. I have no enthusiasm for anything.'

I just started crying. She probably did not understand how she had hurt me just by mentioning that. She did not understand. It was worth everything, healing people with cancer. Did she not have any feelings, no sympathy no humanity? I buried my face in my hands and just hoped she would leave me alone.

'Live is not worth living,' she said.

It was, it was if my husband would get better and I could get back to my old life. But if he would not survive, I would probably live in a pool of misery for the rest of my life, but that still did not mean life was worthless. There would be other people I would harm just by killing myself.

'My husband has cancer,' I blurted out between my tears.

'Oh.'

Was that all she was going to say? I was not sure if she had understood, if she cared. How could someone be human and have no feelings at all. I was full of negative feelings. My whole body felt weak, like there were small particles eating me up from the inside and the outside. My whole legs were tingling, almost shaking. I could do anything anymore. How was I feeling all this pain? I was fed up with this patient that was so dearly trying to help. Without another word I stood up and left to go home. I was planning to just wet my whole bed with tears till I fell asleep from exhaustion. I knew there was nothing that would cheer me up.

And so it was. I lay in my bed, cried the bed full of tears. The next morning, I regretted doing that do myself. I looked horrible. I felt horrible. I even smelt horrible. I rushed under the shower before heading out for work. I was hoping I would not need to say a word to Miss David. I had no motivation, nor the power to do that today. She was heartless. I did not feel like helping her anymore, not that I did not care but I cared more about the other patients. I was not sure about that either. I cared about every human being, everyone should have the same chances and should be seen as equal and be given more than one chance. I was just annoyed at her and wanted to avoid her, for my own good. That was how I was going to put it.

'I am sorry for yesterday,' a voice said from behind.

Flustered, I turned around and guess who was being pushed down the hall in a wheelchair?

'It's ok,' I answered.

I knew I was lying but it was the good kind, I guess. I could not say, 'You really hurt me' in the middle of the hospital hall, where all the other nurses were walking about. I saw her mouth open again, probably to continue the conversation I did not want. I started walking faster, pretending I had not noticed – I had no energy to do this right now. I would rather run away. It was not going to solve anything, but it would prevent causing further problems, but they caught up to shortly after.

'Good morning, Ava,' Grace, one of the other nurses, said.

'Good morning, Grace,' I answered.

'Miss David told me that she desperately wants to talk to you and since my shift is almost over, we could trade off.'

I could not answer anything other than 'yes'. I had no other option right now. Sometimes I really wish I had some luck. I really did not need this right now. I put on my fake smile and tried to be positive.

'Of course.'

'Enjoy your day then,' she said.

And she was off walking down the light blue plastic like floor like a Victoria's Secret model, probably heading home to take a nap.

'I really need to apologize to you for yesterday. I know you are just trying to do your job and only want the best, but sometimes I don't see that.'

'It's ok.'

Why could I not answer with anything other than that?

'I also should have not said the thing about the cancer.'

Well, was it too late to say that now? I would have to give her a second chance. I had no other choice, I guess. I pushed her back to her room.

'How was physical therapy?' I inquired, changing the topic.

'I don't like any kind of therapy.'

What was her problem? Why did she refuse any of the help she was given here.

'You will get used to it over time and it won't go on forever.'

'Mmhh,' is all that came out of her mouth.

I helped her up on her bed, covered her and wanted to leave.

'Will I see you again today?' she asked.

'Most likely.'

I did not want promise anything.

'Please come here before you leave.'

I not going to do that, I left without answering. Was I ?I did not want to make empty promises. I still had not checked her file. I would do that tonight. My phone was buzzing in my pocket; I could feel the vibration throughout my whole body. I should not be taking it to work but when I saw Brice was the caller, the rules did not matter.

'Hey, how are you feeling, how is chemo going, can I do something for you, are you ok, what are the doctors saying, are the nurses being nice to you, is the food ok, do you need anything from home?' Before I could continue, he stopped me.

'Slow down, I am just calling you to tell you that I love you.'

'I love you to.'

He paused for quite a long time.

'You're at work, so I am going to hang up now.'

'No, don't. Tell me how you are doing. Work can wait.'

'I am surviving, but I am going to go now. Byee.'

'Bye.'

Ee ... and I was already cut off the line. What kind of phone call was that? I am sure that was not what he had intended to call for. He was just afraid to tell me. Or ... I don't know, I could not read his mind. I was just trying to.

I looked at the floor as I went from one of the patient's rooms to the next. I was not working the way I should be. I almost missed the vein of one patient's arm when I took their blood. I was going to lose my job if I continued like this.

SUPPORT SYSTEMS

I was packing up my stuff and was contemplating going to see Miss David. I did not want to let her down and I did not want to go either. But I pulled myself together. It's your job, you need to do it, I tried to tell myself. You love this job despite all the downsides. Just go. I was walking out when I turned around and went to look for her file. It had just hit me that I desperately had to read it. I took it out and just took some pictures. So, I could be out of there as quick as possible. I could look through it at home. It wasn't quite allowed but I was doing this for her, and I did not want to steal personal Information from her. It wasn't like I was trying to do something illegal with it. I tried to justify what I was doing and somehow, I managed, and I was off.

Looking all around me, acting as I had just robbed a bank, I tiptoed into the room, hoping that she was asleep, and I could leave without saying a word. But she must have had amazing hearing or be a very light sleeper, cause she sat up and looked at me, as if it took her a while to realize where she was and who was there.

'How are you feeling?' I asked, since it seemed to be the right thing to ask at the moment. Plus, it was the only thing that came to my mind.

'I don't know, but I thought you weren't going to come anymore today.'

'I could not give empty promises just like that.'

'I need to talk to you about your husband's cancer,' she said.

I was in shock. I stood stock still and did not move for a while. What was this about?' Maybe she had some sense, and she would apologize?

'Yes,' I said.

What did she want to tell me.

'As I have already told you. I have been working on a drug that should basically eat up the tumours. It should trigger the cell from destroying itself in a similar way as chemo does. It is just a lot more effective, and the surrounding cells should stay intact. I am sure you understand.'

'But how is that going to help me?' I enquired.

'Your husband has a very advanced stage of cancer, which is hard to treat with chemo, right? If there is a way you could get the drug from my pharmaceutical company, we could use it to treat your husband. There is one downside though. The pills have not been tested nor approved yet.'

'But what if they don't work?' I asked. I was sceptical, it felt like I was she was some witchcraft lady or something. This was a bad idea; I should just go home. She was crazy, wasn't she? How did I know that she was telling the truth? Maybe she was just making everything up. But I was intrigued, I was desperate. I wanted him, I needed him. I needed him more than he needed me.

'It's a risk. I don't know. I just trust my work. Just think about it,' she said, in a timid voice.

'I will.'

There was no way I was going to give my husband unapproved drugs! This lady could be full of shit anyway. I was just going to be nice to her, tell her I did not want her help but thank her that she thought of me. That was what I was going to do.

'I should be on my way home,' I said.

'Ok. Think about it.'

I left her room as quickly as I could. I could not hold myself together anymore, just the bare thought of my husband not having a very high chance of getting through all of this safely. It made me want to turn back time. I got in my car and just cried. The entire outside world did not exist for moment. I heard the car door open, but I did not even turn my head. I was so inside my thoughts, so engulfed by my sadness. I felt someone grab my hand and wipe tears off of ma face. I did not even budge. It was Leanne, she worked with me. I had known her forever. We had gone to nursing school together, I had been her maid of honour and she had been mine. She knew that I was not doing well. She could see it. It was like I did not need to tell her anything and she would just know. She stroked my shoulder and kissed my forehead, just like she used to. She adjusted her position in the passenger seat and looked me up and down, like she was scanning my emotions and state of mind.

'What's going on with you Ava?', Leanne asked.

'it's nothing,' I managed to blurt out.

'It's clearly not nothing,' she said.

She squeezed my hands.

'Mmm,' I just wanted to be left alone.

'Look. How about I drive you home?'

I climbed over into the passenger seat, and she got out the door, walked around the car and got into the driver seat. We drove in silence apart from her humming along to the music from the radio. We turned into my driveway, then we got out of the car and she opened the door for me. She grabbed me and walked me up to my apartment. She sat me down on the sofa, covered me with a blanket and said something in a low town. She left and within no time I had closed my eyes and fallen asleep. My body had been so deprived of sleep, my body had probably shut down and made me go asleep. I could smell coffee brewing when I opened my eyes. I followed the smell to the kitchen. For a split second I thought I had woken up from a nightmare. I was relived till I realized it had all been reality. Leanne was standing upright in the kitchen, filling two mugs with coffee. Had she stayed here all night? She must have. As if she was not there, I walked to the fridge and opened it. It was full of groceries. I had not gone to the store in a long time, or had I just forgotten? I was too busy with other stuff.

'Good morning,' she said. She turned her head at me and probably expected a reaction. But I needed a moment to gather myself.

I just looked at her as if she were a ghost haunting my house. I sat down at the table and took a sip of the coffee that was placed on the table. She handed me a plate with two buttered toasts and sat down across from me. Where Brice usually would sit. And I already felt the tears coming, why did I need to be emotional about every tiny thing. Why was everything tied to emotions. It felt like the more times I cried, the easier the tears came.

She came around and hugged me from the back.

'Everything is going to be fine.'

'Mmh.' I was not convinced.

'Do you want to talk about it?'

'I don't know.'

'Can you at least tell me what's up with you?'

'Brice has cancer.' I cried out.

She hugged me again, this time harder, and did not let go for a while. I felt a bit of weight lifted off my shoulders. It helped saying out loud.

'I am so sorry,' she told me.

'Thank you.'

'But you need to get yourself together. This won't help you, nor will you be helping him in this way.'

'I know.'

She let go of me and sat down across from me again.

'Have you told your parents?' she asked.

Shit. I did not even think of that. Was I going to have to do that? I did not want to. I did not feel like telling anyone. Only days had gone by without him and it already felt like years had passed.

'No.'

'Well, don't worry about that now. You'll get the chance to do that.'

Now she messed my mind up even more. I knew she was not trying to, but I did not want to talk to my parents. I did not really want to talk about it at all. I just wanted it all to go away like nothing had ever happened. She drove me to work, and we both started our shifts like normal, apart from the sympathetic glances she gave me during the day. The only thing that had motivated me was that tomorrow I would be able to go visit my husband and just pull him into my arms and feel his warmth against mine. On my lunch break I went to sit outside so I could just take some time for myself, and then I remembered the file. I took out my phone and went through the photos. The part with her weight, age, gender, name and whatever else I had already seen. I skipped it. On the next page although I read that she had been in the North Psychiatric Institution for five weeks. In the description box or whatever you wanted to call it, I read that she had been there cause she had been suffering a severe trauma due to a murder she had witnessed. Was that the reason why she wanted to kill herself? Because she could not forget the things she had experienced? Was she afraid that some gangster was out for her? On the next page I read about her fall. It described stated that she had fallen out of the window from the 6th floor and had landed on a garbage bin on the side of the street. She had been admitted to the hospital immediately afterwards. It sounded like it was an accident, but I think she was trying to kill herself. It made more sense to my eyes. At the bottom I read the address of the building where she had jumped. It was quite a fancy neighbourhood. I guess she was not too badly off. I swiped to the next picture. There were the contacts of her parents. It was a record of an operation – Laparoscopy – she had had as a kid and the list of shots she had been given. I instantly dialled one of the numbers without thinking it over at all. It rang but before someone answered I panicked and hanged up.

I did not know what I should think of her anymore, maybe what she was going through was harder than I thought. I deleted the photos on my phone. I did not want anyone finding them. Including myself, it was not fair to be snooping around in someone's personal business. My lunch was almost over so I ate my pasta salad which Leanne had made relatively quickly. I had not been exactly hungry. I just ate something for the sake of eating something. The afternoon passed quickly. I was more motivated than the last few days cause I knew how I would be rewarded this evening. In the car I sang my lungs out from the joy I had. I walked into the hospital and went straight to his room. I opened the door slowly in order not to wake him in case he would be sleeping. He would need that rest. He was awake but he had not noticed me yet. I went in slowly and gave him a hug, then he finally realized I was there.

'Hey,' he said in a voice that made my heart melt.

'How are you doing my dear?'

'I am surviving.'

I kissed him on his forehead and held his hand and just sat there looking him in the eyes, trying to figure out what he was thinking. But I could not exactly make it out.

'What are the doctors saying to you?'

'Nothing important.'

'Just tell me. Most of the things doctors say have some sort of importance.'

'Here we go again. You always need to know everything.'

'I just want to help you,' I said, slightly angrily.

'I don't want to talk to you if you are being like this.'

'Like how?'

'You know what I mean, just try to listen to yourself.'

'Try to listen to yourself. You can't even tell me what the doctors are saying.'

'It's for the best.'

'No its not. How do you know what is best for me?'

'I want you to leave if you are like this.'

'Sure.'

I stood up and with a tear covered face I left his room. I tried to cover my face in order to cover my tears. This was not what I had been looking forward to. I called my sister. I needed to talk to someone familiar that would not judge and would just let me say whatever I needed to. I was so mad. He had just sent me away as if I was worthless trash no one wanted. He did not want me. I just wanted to help him.

'What's up?' she asked.

'Brice has gotten cancer.'

There was silence.

'Are you being serious or are you messing with me?'

'I would never joke about something like that.' What was she thinking? Was I such a bad person?

'I'm sorry. I was just making sure.'

'I feel so terrible.'

'Should I come over?'

'Are you kidding? It's a thirteen-hour ride here. Are you being serious? You have your kids to take care off, just don't worry.'

'I am off work for four days.'

'It's too much to ask for', inside of me I was hoping for her to show up at my front door.

'You can never ask too much from me.'

'I can, already calling you at this hour.'

'You can call me anytime. Hunter is anyway watching some sort of family movie with the Callie and Ken.'

'I don't know what I should do.'

'I know the two f you will get through this. Have you told Mom and Dad yet? '

'No.' How come that was the first thing everyone thought about.

'Have you told anyone yet?' she asked.

'Well, you know and a colleague from work, and, weirdly enough, a patient of mine.'

'You need to tell them. Do *his* parents know?'

'I don't know.'

That had not even crossed my mind. Everyone was concerned about the others, but what about me?

'I'm going to come over,' she insisted.

'No, you're not, you've got a family to care for at home.'

'You're family too, and Hunter can manage on his own. The house might get wrecked and the kids might end up only eating pasta and frozen pizza but they will survive. They will probably enjoy it.'

'Are you sure?'

'I am certain.'

'You don't need to come.'

'It is settled. Are you even home yet?'

'No I am still in the car park at the hospital.'

'You should probably slowly make your way home.'

'I know.'

'I will stay on the phone till you get home.'

'You're just too kind to me. You don't need to do that.'

'I want to. I'm your sister. I can be kind when I want to be. I can also be a total ass to you.'

I started the engine of the car.

'I know.'

'When did you finish with work?'

'Around two hours ago.'

'So why are you still at the hospital?'

'I just wanted to visit Brice.'

'I am guessing that did not go all as planned.'

'Well, not exactly. I went in and everything was fine and then he got mad at me and wanted me to leave, so I did.'

'Oh, he's probably just under a lot of stress himself.'

'But I hate it when he keeps things from me.'

'But you always want to know everything. I am sure he has his reasons.'

'Ya, maybe but it is something he has to tell me ...'

'But just imagine being in his situation. Would you want to tell your wife you have cancer?'

'No I wouldn't, but I could not keep it for myself ...'

'It's a difficult situation, you got to see that.'

'I just want to know what the doctors are saying about his cancer. I want to help.'

'I know but maybe you've just got to lay low for a bit and give him some space.'

'I am not sure that I can do that, to be honest.'

There was no way. I could just watch him fade away. I felt like I needed to take action. I needed to do something. I needed some sort of power.

'I know, but you could at least try.'

'Ugh, you're back to your annoying side.'

'I am just trying to help you here.'

'I know but helping can be annoying.'

'You just said it yourself. Brice might be a bit annoyed with you always trying to help more than the possible. I caught you red-handed girl.'

'But he needs it now.'

'He does, but maybe just in a different way than you think. Just imagine yourself in that situation.'

'Ugh.'

'Want to talk about something completely different?' she asked.

'Doesn't matter.'

She changed the topic. 'How is work going?'

'Everything was perfect until this shit started with Brice.'

'Why?'

'There is this one patient, the one that knows he has cancer. I can't quite get smart about her. I think she tried to commit suicide and she keeps asking me to help her to kill herself.'

'Oh, my God!'

'She also wants me to make my husband a guineapig to test her pills.'

'What do you mean?'

So much for another topic. I could not talk about something else. Cause whatever we would talk about, it would lead back to this. Everything was connected.

'She used to work in a pharmaceutical company where she was developing some sort of drug to treat cancer.'

'And why not?'

'She is crazy. I don't even know if what she is saying is true. She was in a psychiatric ward cause of a trauma. Do you realize how shady all of it would be? It's not realistic. Like she might just be making all of this up.'

'Why not call this pharmaceutical company. Would be worth a try. Wouldn't it be?'

'I don't know. I 'll think about it.'

'I wish I could talk longer, but my phone is about to die.'

'Don't worry.'

'Do you want me to call you back?'

'No need.'

'OK, bye. Don't cry to much. Text me when you get home safely.'

'Bye Thank you Aline.'

That felt good. I just loved her; she was practically the opposite of me. And for once I had not hated driving all that much. I was almost home when I saw a drive-through and I thought ff this I am going to get a milkshake. It was the right decision. It was so sweet it was almost sickening, almost disgusting but just almost. I got home, sat down on the couch, and checked my phone. There was a text message from an unknown number.

Hello, you tried to phone me without leaving a message. I was wondering if you just dialled the wrong number or if you are trying to get hold of me. Greetings.

Ah was this the number I called that I found in Miss David's records? Maybe. I responded:

Hi, my name is Ava Collins I am a nurse at the New York Presbyterian Hospital. I reckon this is the mother of Mia David. She fell from a window and landed here with some medium-severe injuries. I was just wondering if you knew.

I was not sure if my message made sense. But I rewrote it a few times and I was just fed up. I was just going to send it the way it was. I did not know if what I was doing was correct or morally ok, but I was doing it no matter what. I thought it was for the best. What else was I supposed to do? I basically had no other choice. Well, there was always a choice, but well. ... I put my phone away and tried to justify what I had just done. At least it was distracting me from everything else that had been happening.

CHERRY CHEESECAKE SECRETS

I heard the doorbell ring and there was no doubt that it was Aline. Who else? No one else would be ringing the doorbell at this time. And she would not stop ringing. No one would have so little respect as to ring and knock the door nonstop. It just made it more clear to me that it was her. I wanted to stay where I had fallen asleep and not get up to open the door. But eventually my ears where hurting maybe I should give her a key. That would solve the problem or create another. I opened the door and was greeted with a warm hug and a bottle of wine.

'Hey, ma dear,' she whispered in my ear. You let me wait for quite a time in front of the door. For God's sake, it is freezing out.'

'You ruined my ears. Now I am going to get early onset deafness!'

'I was just getting you out of bed.'

'Sure.'

'You're off work today?

'Yes, or I would be late.'

'Then hurry up. We're going out.'

'Where?'

'Just get ready.'

'I wanted to go visit Brice.'

'You can later, first we're going to have fun.'

'Do I want to have fun?'

'Everyone wants to have fun.'

'Mmm ... sure.'

I went upstairs and changed out of my work clothes I had not been bothered to take off. I came down and saw her eating my favourite chocolate from the drawer.

'What exactly do you think you are doing?'

'Enjoying myself while I am waiting for you.'

'Take your hands off my chocolate.'

'Says who?'

'Me, obviously.'

'Let's go,' she said, ignoring the fact that she had done something close to illegal.

I took the chocolate away and put it away in the cupboard. I grabbed my handbag, and I was off to do something I probably did not really feel like at the moment. But this was my sister for you, she was always full of energy. Always trying to make the worst situations fun. She started her car and I tried to guess what we were doing.

'Now tell me, where are we going? I asked.

'No way Jose.'

'Yes way, you're going to tell me right now, otherwise.'

'Otherwise what?'

I stared tickling her and she stared shrieking. She started jumping up and down so much that she hit her head on the car roof. She looked at me.

'I thought we were over this stage,' she said.

And she started getting her revenge on me. I had not laughed like that in a long time.

'I thought you were. I never was.'

'Let's get going.'

'Where are we going?' I asked her again.

'Somewhere.'

'Oh, I know that place so well.'

'Do you?'

'Could you just tell me for God's sake.'

'I won't tell you, for anyone's sake.'

'Please, otherwise I am not coming.'

'You're not moving from my side.'

'You can't order me around.'

'Sure I can, I am your older sister. I have all the right.'

'Ugh.'

I had forgotten how strenuous being with her could be.

'Giving up the fight?'

'Never against you.'

'We'll see about that soon enough.'

We drove, and after a while I knew where we were going.

'Are you serious?'

'About what.'

'Are we literally just driving to Niagara falls?'

'Maybe.'

'That's a six hour or seven-hour drive and you just drove all night.'

'I don't care.'

'You're too much to handle.'

'I know that you love that place.'

'I do, thank you.'

'Oh, don't worry. I want to go there myself.'

We passed the rest of the journey chatting about nothing, staring at the scenery and sometimes lapsing into silence. When we arrived we parked the car and, I started to run to the falls. The falls had been so well implanted in my memory it had seemed like we had just been there. She came from behind and grabbed my hand and twirled me around.

'You're acting just as you did when we visited them when you were a small girl.'

'You were not much bigger.'

'But smarter.'

Oh gosh, she would really never change. We walked along the falls. I loved how the mist of water hit my face. It was so refreshing. I was always so surprised by how big and powerful the falls were. To me they had a certain peace. Maybe it was because they were opposites that they went together so well. We walked alongside the falls and then leaned against the railing looking over the falls. Aline turned to and just gave me a look.

"So was that fun?", she asked.

"Something like that."

"Common."

"Ok, it was fun."

"Do you think you are ready to tell mom and dad."

"I want to be, but I don't think so."

"I know you can.'

We sat down on a bench and talked about old times. We started giggling about the thought that we used to fight over the last ice cream in the freezer. We talked about how I had met Brice and she had hated him. It felt good to be seeing her again and her positiveness spread a bit into my direction.

On our way back I fell asleep in the car. I was so exhausted. I had been so sleep deprived I could just not keep my eyes open even if I tried too. I wondered how she did it. She had been driving for so many hours and did not show the slight bit of tiredness. What was she taking? I wanted it too. She woke me up and we were not home but at our parents' house. Now I knew what she was planning.

'We're not going in there.'

'I told them we were coming for dinner.'

'You just want me to tell them about Brice's cancer.'

'I won't make you but I want you too.'

I started to feel nervous. I could not do it. I had just been able to clean out my mind and here I was about to mess it all up again. It was like someone had just sorted all the cutlery and then it had all fallen on the floor, and one could start from the beginning.

'I don't want to,' I said.

'Yes you do. You're the one who always wants to know everything and now you can tell them something simple.'

'it's not simple.'

'Well, its manageable. So get your ass out of my car and we're going in. Remember you told me you couldn't keep things to yourself. Well, here is your chance to speak.'

She tugged my arm and I tried to not let her pull me out of the car, even though I knew she would win eventually. I gave up but tried not to show her. I knew she was right about telling them, but I just did not want to. I would never have come here if she had basically not kidnapped me and brought me here. I could not tell them. They thought my life was perfect and now

141

there was a dent, a dent that I had to tell them about. I was horrified about telling them. What were they going to think? I knew they would just want to help, but I did not want that. Again, I wanted to be left alone.

'Oh come on, don't be so stubborn.'

She rang the front doorbell, and it still made the same familiar sound from out childhood. Our mom opened the door and hugged both of us at the same time and covered us in kisses. It smelt just like it always did. You could smell the floral cleaning detergent that my mother used in excess, the old furniture and of course, dog. Altogether it smelt like home.

'I am so glad to see you. You both look exhausted. Come in, come in! How are you both doing? How are your kids? How are both of your handsome husbands doing? I made your favourites. Are you hungry?' She could continue asking questions and I would not even remember the first. I thought it was so cute but what she did not realize is that like this she only received an answer to ten percent of her questions cause she did not even give us a chance to open our mouths for longer than a few seconds.

'Slow down mom, we just got here.'

'I'm sorry. I am just so excited to see you. You have to come visit more often.'

'Like mother, like daughter,' I said.

They both had their way with run-on sentences, speaking without an end in sight.

'What did you say, hun?'

'Oh nothing, just happy to see you.'

My sister let out a small laugh and a smile. At least she had gotten what I had said. Our dad was sitting at the table when we came into the kitchen.

'You guys made me wait for dinner.'

Then he stared laughing. He would never change. He would always have his own sense of humour.

'Oh, did we?'

'Your mom has been going crazy the whole day knowing that you two were coming here tonight.'

'Now don't exaggerate things,' my mom told him.

'What are you standing there, aren't you going to give me a hug or is that too much to ask for?' he asked.

'What do you think?' my sister reasoned with me.

'I think after insulting us for making him wait he doesn't deserve it.'

We both went over to him and hugged him.

'I love you girls soo much', he said as we were squeezing him to pieces.

'We love you too dad,' we said at the same time.

Before we could even sit down our mom was setting plates and plates of food out. It smelt so good. Dad had not been exaggerating.

'Are you trying to make us fat?' my sister asked.

'You both have a bit of room for some food.'

'Oh mom.'

'It's not Christmas,' I said.

'It's also not a normal day,' she replied.

'It is.'

The two of us looked at each other, shaking our heads. During the dinner my sister, Alinegave me a kick on my shin. I tried not to scream but I could have. I felt it burning from pain. I knew she was telling me it was time to tell my story. But I was going to procrastinate for as long as I could. I was afraid, even though I knew there were was no reason to be. I knew they would be supportive, and they would immediately want to help, but for some reason there was still something inside of me that did not want to tell them. I think Aline had lost her patience with me. She had never been patient. I wonder how her kids handled it. How she handled the kids. The food was just like I had imagined, home-cooked, the best. The cherry cheesecake that she put down after we finished all our veggies looked to die for. But it did not let me forget why we were there, and as if my sister could read my mind she said:

'I think Ava has something to tell you guys.'

I looked daggers at her. I wanted to kill her at that moment. Could she not just hold her horses and keep quiet? These were my affairs, not hers. Just let me handle it or was that not possible?

'Oh, are you pregnant my dear? That's great.'

'No, I am not.'

My mom sighed. She desperately wanted to have more grandchildren. I just wish she would not have said that. It made telling her ten times harder.

'So tell me, your sister just got me excited.'

'It's no news anyone should be excited about,' I said.

'That doesn't change the fact that I want to know it. If it's something bad I want to know it even more. I want to help you if I can. You know that you can tell us everything.'

Again the thing with help.

'I know.' I paused and shifted my eyes towards the floor. I did not want anybody looking at my face right now.

'Brice has cancer,' Aline blurted out.

She would not let me handle my own things, would she? I felt the tears coming I tried holding them back, I had already cried too much about this. I tried not blinking to not let a tear fall down the side of my cheek, but I was unsuccessful. My mom took her napkin and wiped the tears from my face. And looked at my sister, maybe with a bit of anger. She must have been grateful to receive the news but not in the way she would have wanted to.

'You could not let her tell us herself, could you?' she asked my sister.

'I thought she would never get to the point,' she said in her defence. But her expression said everything, she had not intended and felt so bad for it. Just for a moment no one looked in each others' eyes.

'You know that Brice has a family history of cancer.'

'I am sorry. I could just not stand watching anymore. I could not keep my mouth shut.'

I think my dad was shocked and did not know what to do. Surrounded by three emotional women overloaded with feelings. He just sat there in silence looking at us with wide open eyes.

'Do you want to talk about it?' mom asked.

I wanted to say 'no' but I know that my mom wanted a different answer than that. I just said nothing. I managed to stop crying and sit there like an adult should.

'What is there to talk about?' I asked.

'Well how do you feel?' she countered.

'There is no other way then to feel horrible. What do you think?'

'I know, I just want to help?'

'I know?'

'What kind of cancer is it?'

'Colorectal cancer stage four'

My mother, with her mouth open, started crying. Soon all of us were covering our plates of desert with tears. My sister started eating her tart and I followed suit. I needed the kick of dopamine that the sugar was hopefully going to give me.

'The pie makes me feel better,' I stated.

'All I can taste is the salt from my tears,' my sister added with food falling out of her mouth.

'You girls are staying the night, aren't you?'

'I need to go see Brice,' I said firmly.

'We're staying,' my sister corrected.

'We can, but we have to see him first thing tomorrow.'

'I think you should stay. It is still a three-hour drive to New York.' My dad had at least lost his silence.

'But we are leaving first thing,' I exclaimed.

'If you get me up and you drive.'

And so we stayed the night. Not exactly what I wanted, but I still felt good there. It was a secure place, and it was like it used to be, me and my sister sharing a bed. And, dear God, I slept well.

'Good morning.'

I hugged her, and she just moaned. I knew she did not want to get up but then she licked my face.

'YWee, what were you thinking?'

What on earth was that suppose to be? I was definitely not into such a thing. I did not have a fetish for people's tongues.

'Oh, nothing.'

She was soo weird. Just forget it, I tried to tell myself. It never happened. It was just a mirage.

'Ok, let's go.'

She jumped out of bed, pushing me away. There was her energy. Maybe I did not need to drive after all. And what did I expect, our mother was already in the kitchen and my dad pottering around her.

'I made you guys some food to take with you.'

'You're too much, mom.'

'You're going to need it on that long ride.'

She gave us a bag, and a few hugs. Almost not letting us leave but eventually we managed to say our goodbyes and get out of the house. I know she only wanted the best, but she could let me go. And guess what? I did not need to drive cause Aline did not trust my driving skills. The whole ride I was just trembling cause I was anxious about what was awaiting me in the hospital. The closer we got, the worse it got, and Aline placed her hand on my leg to stop it from shaking but it did not help.

'Why are you so scared?' she asked.

'I'm not.'

'Don't lie to me.'

'Well, I don't know.'

'You will be fine, trust me. He loves you and you love him, no matter what. That's all that matters. Trust me. Just this once.'

'Don't be so full of clichés.'

'You are a cliché,' she told me.

'Not really. I wish I was normal,' I replied.

'Normal is boring. Now, just go in.'

'I am.'

'You were the one who wanted to leave this early in the morning.'

'I know.'

I could not handle her anymore and opened the car door and walked straight up to the hospital. I wanted to see him so terribly so that is what I was going to do; there was nothing else that

I could do. It could not get worse than it already was, could it?
And there I stood in front of his bed, the man I loved so dearly
lying there as if I was a stranger he did not care about.

'I told my parents.' was the only thing that came to my mind.

'What?'

'I told them you had cancer.'

'What?' he asked again.

'Are you deaf? I told my mom and my dad that you are in the
hospital and have been diagnosed with cancer.'

'Why would you do that?'

Everyone wants me to tell them and now it was not good. I
was confused and mad at everything and everyone. I was about
to explode from the rage that was cooking in me.

'Cause it's the right thing to do, at least that is what I thought.'

'Do you realize that I have not told mine yet? You know what
kind of drama you're going to create with this?'

'If you would have talked to me then this would have never
happened. But you just sent me away. What were you expecting? That you could keep all of this your personal little secret?
You probably did not even want to tell me. You're going to need
to tell them eventually. '

'Its not the right time.'

'It never will be the right time,' I replied.

'It's all your fault. Why did you tell them? I thought I knew you.'

'I thought I knew you too. If you want to blame it on someone, blame Aline, not me.'

'Why should I blame your sister? Clearly you're the one in-
tertwined in all this. You said it.'

'Actually, no she did, but it was the right thing.'

'Well, you told her then.'

'Do you expect me to keep all of this a secret and not talk to
anyone? Don't you think this is hard on me to? It's not all just
about you.'

'You could ask.'

'What is there to ask? I have the right to talk to people. Plus,
how should I ask if you don't talk to me? If I asked you a ques-

tion it's always, "Don't worry, its nothing important, you don't need to know,".'

'But you can't just go around telling people anything.'

'But it's not anything.'

'Sometimes it is better if people don't know.'

'And most of the time the truth comes to light at some time. You think no-one would have noticed. It is only fair telling your parents. Were you just going to fade away and think no one would notice? In case you haven't noticed yet, I care for you. I care for you a lot. All I am trying to do is help you. I just want you to get better. But I am sorry, ignoring the fact that you are ill is not going to help us in this situation.'

'I don't want to tell my parents.'

'Do you think I wanted to tell mine? You're acting like a child. Tell them now, just call them. Otherwise, they will know it from somebody else. Tea travels fast, so you'd better hurry.'

'Do you see what kind of situation you've put me in?'

'I don't.'

'You're ridiculous.'

'Call them now.'

'I'm not going to.'

'Then I will ask my sister to.'

'How about you do it?'

'Just call them,' I screamed.

I could no longer control my temper. I was wandering back and forth from one wall to the other thinking of what to say, what to do. I did not know. I was not prepared for a situation like this. A nurse opened the door and I turned to face her.

'Everything ok in here?' she asked.

'Fine, thank you,' we answered, in unison.

I took his phone from the night table and called the number and put him on speaker. I sat down and waited. I could not recall being like this to him. Was I being too harsh? Was I being mean? I did not like myself like this, but emotions and actions came before thoughts at the moment, whether I liked it or not. And then his mom picked up the phone and the walls around me came crashing down. What on earth had I done? What if he had done the same to me? I would have wanted to pull his insides out. But he stayed calm. He just would not keep his fiery eyes off me.

'Hello, Brice are you there?'

'Mmh'

'You haven't called us in a long time. Have you been under a lot of stress at work?'

'A bit.'

'You and Ava need to come over again, me and dad miss you.

'We will.'

'Is she there with you? I want to say hi to her.'

'She is,' he uttered.

My hand was shaking as I took the phone from him. I even thought of just hanging up. But I could not do that. I felt like I was frozen:

'Hello, Barbara. How are you doing?'

'Great ... a bit weak. What about you?'

'Fine, thank you.'

'Good to hear.'

'Should I hand you back to Brice? I got to go.'

'Sure dear, have a wonderful day. Look out for my boy.'

'I will. Bye.'

I handed the phone back, scared for what would come next. His mom's ex-husband had died from cancer and I knew that this was a sensitive subject and I knew she would be upset about him not telling her earlier. But what was there left for me to do? It felt like everything was out of my power at that moment.

'I hope you cherish your wife, boy.'

'Of course I do.'

'So why did you call?'

'Oh for no reason.'

'You only call if something is up.'

'No I don't.'

'Where are you at the moment?'

Brice paused and did not say anything for quite a while. I would not have known what to say either. I started to feel really bad for what I had done. Why was I so stupid sometimes? I saw him swallow and look at me with desperation. I sat down on his bed and held his hand.

'Are you still there?'

'Yes.'

'What's wrong? I know something is up. I'm your mother. Just tell me I am sure it is nothing all to bad'

'I have cancer,' he whispered.

I heard her crying over the speaker and I just felt bad for making him do this.

'Are you ok?' she managed to get out.

'I am fine, mother.'

'We're coming there right away.'

'You don't need to worry.'

'There is no use in telling me that.'

'Have you told Ava?'

'Of course.'

Well of course, it took him quite a while to tell me about it. More like forcing it out of him.

'Good, what about your daughter?'

He turned the speaker off and put it to his ear. I smacked his leg and gave him an angry look. I went outside the room and let out a scream. What was that suppose to mean. What was she taking about? I felt betrayed, I felt stupid. Did he really have a daughter that I did not know about. Sorry but what the ff. I have known him for years. Had I just misunderstood? I have been married to him for 8 years. What, how? How could I trust him by just hearing this? I could not, there was no way I could deal with this. I stamped back in the room, and he just shushed me as if I meant nothing at all to him. What the hell was he thinking? I was his wife, and he had a quite big secret that he had been keeping from me. I must have just understood something differently. No. There was no way this could be a misunderstanding, no way. I know what I heard. Wait if he has a daughter? Then did he have an affair, or did he have her before we met? He did not have a child when he was seventeen or eighteen or did he?

And why would he tell his mother and not his wife? That was not right. Did he trust her more? If she had known, why did she not tell me? I had thought I knew everything, I thought I could trust him fully and I thought he trusted me fully. I started to sweat, my hands were shaking. I felt like throwing up. I felt so uncomfortable. My heart started to beat faster, and I could almost not stand upright. The thought was killing me.

But as I was seeing that was not the case. I did not even know if I could forgive him for not telling me. And he was still on the phone. I was soo close to just pulling that damn thing out of his hand and running out and clearing this all up with his mom. Had she known that he was keeping this from me? Were they all on this and I was the only one who did not know what was going on? I thought nothing could break us, but we were decomposing bit by bit, leaving a trail of crumbs that were sinking down to hell. I started to feel really hot, and I felt cool drops of sweat drip down my forehead. I took off my sweater and sat down on the chair trying to fan my face with my hand. 'You're not having a mental breakdown, you're not having a mental breakdown,' I tried telling myself but there was no use. I was in the middle of breaking down. How could he not tell me something like this? What was he thinking, probably nothing at all. And I got even more annoyed cause I could only hear his side of the call. It could not be, I just must of heard something else.

'I know.'

'You know I have not had any contact.'

'There is no point.'

'I think that would mess everything up.'

'Just think of her foster parents.'

'I cant.'

'I know I should have.'

I could not make out what they were saying but I knew what they were talking about and that made me even more furious than I was. I could not even listen anymore. My face was covered in sweat and tears. I couldn't take this anymore: I stood up and walked to the window to hold my head out to get some fresh air, but that did not help either, to be honest. The air did not feel any better than inside the room. I was expecting it to be cool, fresh and clean, but it wasn't. All I inhaled was the smoke from some random person who was smoking down in the courtyard.

'Honey, I can explain.'

He had hung up and was now looking like I was a murderer or something. I was the victim here, how the hell could he be doing this to be? Did I really deserve this? I was certain now that life was unfair.

'You'd better.'

'Look, there is nothing to worry about ', he exclaimed.

'No there is not at all ... you only have a daughter I did not know anything about and wait, ya you have cancer. Nothing to worry about, nothing at all. Its always the same with you. Always.'

'Look, I have a daughter, but I have not seen her in years. I have had no contact.'

'Still does not mean that you should not tell me.'

I had to turn away I could not look at him. How was it possible that I did not know this. I could not take this. It was too much.

'Look, when I had her I was very young. I was seventeen. I did not even know I was the father until three years later. What was I meant to do? I just did not feel comfortable telling you. In the beginning, I thought you would leave me. As time went on, I felt that you would get mad for me not telling you earlier. Like you are now. What was I supposed to do? I tried to just push it away, it was not even present to me.'

'You're telling me you just forgot you had a daughter? I don't think so. And you expect me just to take this all in like this. You could have just told me. I trusted you with all my insecurities, faults, mistakes. Everything. And now, how many years later you tell me you have a daughter. That is not exactly nothing.'

I was not even talking anymore, but just straight screaming at him. I could not accept this. I was so loud my own ears were splitting. I just could not.

'I just never found the right time.'

'Like there was never a right time to tell me you had cancer. You just planned on never telling me or what? What is with you and no right time, the time is never going to be perfect cause you don't want it to be. You coward.'

'I don't know.'

he started pulling up his blanket higher and higher.

'Well, you'd better think about it all. I wonder what else I don't know about you.'

'There is nothing else I swear.'

'And why should I believe that exactly?' I cried.

'Cause I am your husband.'

'As if that is a justification. What does that matter if you have been lying all these years, you would have probably lied for many more if your mother had not accidentally exposed you. Or did she think I know.'

'I don't know.'

'You don't know very much today, do you?' I declared.

'You can't do this to me.'

'What?'

'You just acting like I killed someone or something.'

'You lied to me all these years. Is that any better? I cant trust you, so who says you have not killed somebody.'

'What should I have done? if you were in my situation I don't think you would have told me.'

'You should have just told me, how hard would that of been?'

'Why do you have to be like this?' he yelled, and covered his face with his hands.

'I can ask you exactly the same,' I roared. 'I don't even recognize you like my husband anymore,' I added.

'Well, you're not acting like a wife. You're acting like an inhuman monster that was let out of it's cage.'

I did not know what to say anymore, this situation was just too much to handle. I ran out of the room, out of the hospital, to my sister's car. I swung the door open and sat down.

'Let's go.'

'What happened?'

'Just start the car.'

She turned the key of the car and drove home slowly, always looking over to me, probably hoping for some sort of response, but I was not going to give her one. And definitely not if she kept looking over. I hated it when someone did that.

'Tell me what is up,' she said.

'No.'

'Is Brice ok?' she asked.

'Yes?'

'What's wrong?' she asked again. She was not going to take no for an answer.

'Nothing.'

'That's the biggest lie, I have heard today.'

She stopped the car on the side of the road and got out came around the car opened the door and pulled me out of the car.

'If you're not telling you I am not taking you home.'

'You can't do that.'

'You bet I can.'

'No, you wouldn't,' I wept.

'I am a grown woman, and you're acting like a child. I can do whatever suits me best.'

'You can't just abandon me.'

'It's like five-hundred meters to your apartment, it's not like I am leaving you in the jungle.'

And in the time it took me to realize what she had said she had gotten back in the car and had started the engine.

'Brice has a daughter,' I screamed, hoping she would hear.

But she probably didn't; she drove away and I was stuck walking to my apartment. How could she do this to me, and tell me I was acting like a child? Was she not? She could have just accepted that I did not feel like telling her, like an adult. She was older anyway, so she should look after me or was that too much to ask for? My husband has ff cancer and he has a fff daughter. WTF. Really. Why did she have to be so toxic? Like did her ego need to drop me off on the side of the road and make me walk home, what was the point of that? I did not see it. Everyone was abandoning me. When I asked for help I got 'no' and when I just wanted to be left alone everyone was running to me. I put one foot in front of the other, imagining balancing on the white sideline of the road, kicking stones away with all the force I had. I had enough, I started stamping like a little child, but the ground did not move nothing changed. My force did not make the ground move, it just stayed there and did not shake one bit I don't know why that started frustrating me for no reason, had I expected through the ground and end up in China, or what did I expect to happen.

I STILL LOVE YOU

I got home and was thrilled to see her car. I remembered she had no way of getting in my apartment so she would have had to wait for me, which was quite amusing. But she was not waiting in front of the apartment, I wondered where she might have gone. My question was answered shortly after when she came in with a bag of takeout.

'How was the walk?'

'Oh I loved it.'

'Will you tell me what's up now?'

'Mm ...'

'I got Thai food.'

'Are you going to bribe me now?'

'I would never.'

I ended up telling her over my curry that Brice had a daughter. She had asked one million questions that I could not answer, which made me even more frustrated, cause I could have asked them. I had not even asked them to myself. I wanted to know everything, every tiny detail, I did not care how hard it was for Brice to talk about this topic, I just needed to know. Well, of course I cared but I wanted to gain at least a bit of the trust back that I had lost. I was kind of sad to know that my sister had to go home the next day, but I was blessed to be able to have here. When I got up, she was already gone, but she had left me a bottle of red wine on the table. With a note.

If you need to get drunk in the bathtub.

That was so typical of her.

I decided to go to work and see Miss David. I was still curious about her. I arrived and went straight to her room even though

156

I should of done some administration first but fuck that this would annoy me in my mind until I saw her face and was satisfied with myself.

'Good morning, Ms. David how are you feeling today?' I asked her as I entered.

'Better, I still don't see the point but, how is your husband doing?'

'Fine, thank you for asking.'

He was better but wasn't I better; I was swimming in the pool of his lies. The things I did not know about him were like an unclimbable mountain. I wanted to know everything. I don't know why I had thought that I wanted to see Miss David. I felt a bit confused by myself.

I just remembered the text I had sent and took my phone out of my pocket while I left her room, and there it was an answer. I had forgotten it the whole weekend.

Can I call you?
Of course, how about around six when I finish work, I answered.

Work went by fast, I did not do anything extra. I just did what I had to. The bare minimum.

Who knew what was going to come out of this, but it was worth a try. It was exactly 6.00 when I received a call.

'Hello, Ava Collins here.'

'Hello my name is Natasha David, you're Mia's nurse right?'

'Yes I am, I am guessing you are her mother.'

This phone call was feeling soo surreal. I felt so wrong, I had the feeling that I was not doing the right thing.

'That's right, how is she doing?'

'She is recovering fine.'

'What happened?'

'She fell down from a window and broke some bones, suffered from a concussion and internal bleeding.'

'Oh! I didn't know.'

'I am here to answer any questions you might have.'

'Thank you, can we come and visit her?'

'Of course.'

'Thank you for everything. have a nice day.'

'Thank you, bye.'

I did not know, and I did not want to judge but I had a very strong feeling that Miss David had never told her parents what had happened. Well, her mom just admitted such. I just did not want to believe it. I did not know if that should concern me or if it was normal, I had no idea how their family was, and I had just interfered. She was a grown woman. I did not know what her relationship was like towards her parents, maybe what I had done was not correct, but I thought it was the right thing. Even though I was having my regrets I should have asked Miss David about her parents before I contacted them. But done is done. When I got home, I was sitting in my kitchen thinking, phone in my hand, contemplating if I should call my husband or if I should leave it. I wanted to ask how he was doing, I still cared so deeply about him, but on the other hand I did not feel like calling him since he had betrayed me by not telling me his entire past. What else was there that I had no idea about? I just could not trust him fully anymore. I didn't know if I could trust him at all. I started dialling his number but then after the first three numbers I erased them. I was going to wait for him to call me and apologize. Was that smart? That he had cancer made this whole decision a lot harder than it actually would be, but what was there to do? I did not know. I decided to open the bottle of wine and get in the bath it felt like the best thing to do at the moment. I mean I could take the advice from my sister for once. And there I was in the bath laughing at myself, drunk. I was not all too tolerant to alcohol and I had drunk the entire bottle glass by glass. I was soo drunk. I managed to make my way to my bed with a fall in-between but there were no tears, just laughs. I was lucky that I made it out of bed the next morning, cause I pressed snooze like a million times without realizing I had to get my ass to work. But I was fine, I got there without being late, I probably looked like a hot mess express but at least I got there. When I went into the lunchroom I saw Grace, guessed she had the same shift as me today. I did not know how that made me feel.

'How are you doing?'

'Ok.'

'If you need anything just tell me, ok?'

'Thank you.'

She was so kind but there was nothing that she could help me with for the moment. I just needed a time machine or at least the whole truth from my husband and his daughter. Like if she was his daughter what was I to her, if we were ever to meet. I wanted to meet her in some kind of way. Was that ok or was that just weird to want that? I did not know, literally I knew so little. I could not even decide on my own thoughts.

'I was here yesterday and Miss David was asking about you.'

'Really, why?'

'She asked me to talk to you about the drug for cancer for your husband. She is really convinced about it. Do you think she's bluffing?'

'I don't think it is a good idea. I don't know if what she is saying is true. I really can't tell you.'

' You've got nothing to lose and this could be a great opportunity.'

'But what if it goes wrong? What she is telling us might be bogus. Do you realise how surreal this all is?'

'I checked that,. She is actually a chemist at Johnson & Johnson. She is quite far up there, I stalked her on their website a bit. But I could not find her anywhere else.'

'Oh, you're so weird.'

'I was interested.'

'Did you find anything else about her?'

'I am not that creepy.

'Maybe your just a bad stalker.'

'I don't know if I should take that as a compliment or an insult.'

'Your decision.'

'Just talk to her, if not for your sake then for hers.'

'I'll try.'

'Good, ok, sorry, I got to get to work, you too?'

I did not want Brice to be in that trial, I was to afraid, this Mia girl seemed off to me. Especially after the recent call with her mom, something was just not right there. Maybe it was just me but what if it wasn't? I was going to talk to her today for the last time properly and after that I would just continue with normal small talk with her, I was going to end this back and forth with her today.

'Are you up?' I asked quietly, so as not to wake her if she was still sleeping.

'Yes.'

'How are you feeling?'

'The same as always.'

'I wanted to talk to you.'

'Do you want your husband to participate in the study?'

She sat up in her bed and pulled her blanket down to her hips, She seemed excited.

'About that, I don't think it is a good idea. I don't feel comfortable doing it.'

'Why?'

'Well, the drug has not been tested yet, what if it does horrible things? You don't know the side-effects, anything could happen.'

'That's not true: It has been tested in multiple ways and times, just not on humans yet. Of course, there is a risk, but isn't there always?'

'That does not make me feel a lot better about it to be honest.'

'I just want to help.'

'I know, I am just unsure. I just don't think it is a good idea.'

'And I accept that, I don't want to pressure you about it.'

That's what it felt like though, pressure from all sides. Wanting me to do this, say that, be this way or be another. I was tired. Tired of all this. Could I not just open a window and it would all fly right out and I would never have to deal with it again?

'Thank you,' I responded.

'Can I ask how your husband is doing, even though it is none of my business?'

'Of course you can. To be honest I am not sure, he does not talk very openly about it.'

'I guess it is a difficult situation you are in.'

'You can definitely put it that way.'

'I am sorry.'

'Thank you.'

'I know that it can be hard to talk to people that are close to you.'

This was complying with my suspicions from the phone call.

'I know this might sound wrong but I contacted your mom,' I stated.

She lifted her self a bit and adjusted her position, she looked like she was in a lot of pain. She starred at me, he looked shocked to the bone. It was as if something bad had entered in her and I could see anger boiling up in her.

'What?'

'I called her and told her you were in the hospital.'

'Why would you do that?'

'To help you.'

'Are you ff serious lady, do I look like I want to see my mother?'

'I am sorry, forget about it.'

'I cant forget about that, this is not going to end well. Are you serious? How could you do something like that? What if she shows up here now? What do you expect me to do?'

'Sorry.'

I did not know what to say. Only now was I realizing how unfair it was to mix myself up in her personal life. I had not enjoyed it either when she had done the same. Why had I thought it was ok for me to do that? I was not superior to her. I was similar.

'I thought you weren't like all the other nurses I thought you were better. How could you do that? You could have asked me, or at least warned me or I don't know ...' her voice had started to adopt a louder and more forceful tone.

'All I can say is that I am sorry.'

I did not know if I was should be afraid of her, what was she going to do to me?

'Sorry does not change anything for me. Every person is the same, it always is the same ff thing.'

'What do you want me to say?'

'How should I know, maybe you should realize that there is no point for me anymore.'

'There always is.'

'There are always exceptions, and I am an exception. There is no point, I have lost everything. My job, my family, my friends, my dignity, my happiness, my joy, my life and what am I left with? I am left with thoughts that want to kill me, a broken body and money.'

'I am sorry to hear that, but there is always hope. The world is so big there is something out there for you.'

'That is what you think. I got no hope at all.'

'Please.'

It was so hard talking to her, like why did she need to be almost mean and so negative all the time? I did not know what I could tell her that would make her feel good or better and she had some way of making me feel uncomfortable. Maybe she was cold. That could be an explanation.

'You don't even need to try this with me. You don't need to talk me into sense or whatever, you will just get frustrated.'

I just nodded cause what was there to answer to that? What was there left to say at the moment?

'Can you tell my mother not to come, that is the least you can do after getting me in this mess?

'I don't think that is a good idea to be honest with you.'

'Why not?'

'Cause she wants to visit you, she will come whatever I say.'

'Just do it, you can tell her I died, I don't care I just don't want to see her.'

'There is no way that I can do that.'

'Just do it, you got yourself into this.'

'Just tell her I don't want her.'

'I can't tell a mother that.'

'Just do it,' she screamed.

I was not going to do it, if it was the right thing or not. I could not bring myself to call her and tell her that, even if it was not face to face. Had she not said that she had lost her family, this way she could win them back? Or was I thinking wrong?

'I won't, its not fair. Your mother should be able to see you.'

'I am not a child, she's got no rights over me. The one you are being unfair to is me.'

'Of course legally not, but I think morally and ethically it is the right thing to do.'

'I disagree,' she declared.

I left. I did not want to be a part of this discussion anymore, it was too much to handle. I did not want to lose my temper here. I needed some air, she made me crazy. How could someone have such a hard head and not have any hope at all? Like she said, she had money, so she did not worry about getting through life. she had a degree so she could get a job. Of course, there might be some problems with her family and friends but she could just start over, couldn't she? She could move to another country or something. I did not want to believe that there was no solution for her. She might have a few mental issues but those could be therapized, and she would get better in no time. There were so many possibilities nowadays. But she did not even want to get better, that's how it seemed to me. I had to stay professional.

'Hey.'

I was relived at the sound of his voice. It gave me a inner sense of calm.

'You decided to call.'

'Yes, I still love you,' he said.

'Sure, so why did you have to lie to me?' I asked.

'Cause I was afraid.'

'But that is not reason enough to just not tell me all these years.'

'I know but how should I change the past?'

There was some truth in that sentence.

'Build a time machine or something.'

'I know you're hurt, Ava, but I can't change it and I am sorry and I love you and I want you to trust me again. I want everything to go back to how it was. I did not want any of this either.'

'Those are hard ones. I paused to take a breath. How old is she?,' I asked.

'She is seventeen turning eighteen soon.'

'Are you still in contact with her mother?'

'No, the last time I saw or talked to her was when I was 20.'

'Why did you never tell me these thing?'

I felt the tears forming once more. It was not the first time and surely it was not going to be the last. That was certain.

'I don't feel comfortable talking about it. I was afraid ok.'

'Do you know anything about her?'

Something inside of me felt that I wanted to know this girl. I just wanted to take her into my arms and tell her about her dad. I wish I could be some sort of parent figure to her.

'I know that she lives in Harlem with her foster parents.'

'You don't have any contact?'

'Not really. I just send cards every birthday and Christmas with money and all I ever get back is a thank you card. That's it.'

'Oh, what's her name?'

I was not mad at the moment anymore. All I was, was intrigued by this mysterious girl that I kind of was family with.

'Alice.'

I was so interested in this girl. Me and Brice had been thinking about having children, but we were both too busy with our lives and everything so it kind of got lost. Well, now it was off the table anyhow.

'Nice name.'

A smile started to spread across my face between the tears that were falling. The emotional source of the tears was unclear to me. Once more, I was filled with multiple emotions not knowing what to feel.

'Look I am really sorry for not telling you and as I know you will be mad for quite a while, but can you at least come visit me some time soon. I miss you.'

These words filled my heart with everything it had been missing.

'I will.'

'I love you.'

'I love you more', I promised.

'What do you think? Should I tell her I have cancer?' he asked.

'I don't know.'

'My mom wants me to tell her.'

'What are the doctors saying.'

'They're not sure if chemo working.'

My mouth fell open, the emotions started to change and fear came over me. It was like the split second of happiness had been engulfed by distress.

'What, what are they going to do?'

'I don't know.'

I was crying once again, What did this mean? Was he not going to get better?

'Are you going to get better?'

'Don't worry dear.'

'I am.'

'I am really tired so I am going to hang up.'

I did not want to hang up. I knew that soon the soothing sound of his voice would be gone.

'Bye, I love you.' He ended the call.

And I was gone again. I just wanted to hear his voice. It was like I was given time with him but then it was taken away or I was just cut off. I really missed him, the old him. I wanted to go and visit him, but I couldn't. I needed to go to bed to get up for the early shift tomorrow. I, however, could not find sleep. I was constantly thinking about his daughter and what I wanted to do, and then there was Miss David's mother who was coming to visit. I did not know what to think about that either to be honest. And then the fear of losing my husband completely just came creeping up and that is how I ended up crying myself to sleep once again.

Work was going fine till I started calling in visitors and I called for a visitor for Miss David. What had I done? I saw an elderly

165

woman get up out of a chair. She was wearing a pair of jeans, a blue, white and red-checkered shirt, and she had high boots on. It was not exactly the outfit that I associated with that kind of person, but she was killing the outfit to be honest. I introduced myself and brought her to Miss David's room. She gave me a huge hug and thanked me and I just thought maybe I did the right thing. I was curious and afraid at the same time about how the meeting would end. I tried to drop her off in front of the room, keeping some security distance. However, I walked away slowly while trying to listen to their conversation. All I could hear was the mom asking her why she had just cut them off, and I know Miss David was mad cause I heard her tell her mom it was her fault and she did not want to see her.

But I was already being suspicious enough. I could not stand there like that anymore and I had to move ... their voices were lost in the air. I really wondered what had happened. Maybe I would get the chance to ask. I would try; I was so nosy even though it was none of my business but I almost wanted make it my business, as weird as that sounds. An hour later I just went to the bathroom so I could pass her room to see if her mom was still there, but she wasn't. Should I go in and talk to her? Should I wait till the fire had set a bit? I did not want to be too intrusive. But I could not wait so after my trip to the bathroom I went in, I just needed to ask. My curiosity had overcome me.

MORE PROBLEMS OR SOLUTIONS

'Good morning Miss David, how are you feeling today?'

'Horrible, after the stunt you made.'

'Sorry.'

'Getting my mother here, how could you do that to me?'

'She is your mother.'

I was kinda getting what I wanted, and that made me feel good. And even more on fire cause I wanted to know. I felt adrenalin running through my veins, these kind of things excited me.

'I hate her, I left my home as soon as I could and never went back, I cut off all the contact I had with them completely.'

'Why?'

'Lets say, she ruined things in my life and let's say she is a total bitch and that's no ff understatement.'

'I am sorry to hear that, but don't you think you could forgive her one day?'

'No way.'

I wanted to dig deeper. I wanted to know the whole story.

'Why not, I am sure she just wanted the best for you?'

'I am sorry but she changed her boys as often as she changed her underwear. She slept with my ff boyfriend. I am sorry, a mother does not do that.'

My mouth fell open, that I had to close it with my right hand. This sounded like a drama. I was not sure that she was telling the truth. I think there was more than one side to this story.

'Are you sure?' I asked.

'No but I think it was that way, even though she denies it.'

That makes a difference to me.

'Oh.'

'Look she never understood me. I felt like I was always being attacked by her and I never felt comfortable. It felt like whatever I did it was wrong but she could do whatever she wanted and it was right.'

'Don't you think she just wanted the best for you?'

'No.'

'Why not?'

'She was selfish; she was never happy with what I wanted. I had the feeling she was envious of the life I had. She wanted me to live like she did, follow her past but I think it was cause she did not want me to achieve more than she ever did.'

'But what about the rest of your family?' I think this was more of a mess than I could have imagined. I did not know how I should feel about it. The more I thought about it the more I realized it might have been a mistake contacting her mother. Had I just made her life harder than it already was? Was I bringing more hardship for her?

'My sister was the exact way my mother wanted her to be. She would do everything mom wanted her to. In her eyes, she was perfect. My life was not approved of, so my sister automatically did not like me. My brother was several years older, how should I put it, he wanted attention from his friends and made me do things I did not want to. And there was my dad, I don't even know. Just imagine having no one to talk to. There was no one I could trust, I always felt like they were out for me or for money. Look my parents were not the good old neighbour in a white house with a trimmed front lawn. We lived in a trailer park. My dad had been in prison. I was the first one in the family to go to university. „I was shocked about this girl, how much was there I did not know about her? So much had not expected. I was happy that my relationship with my parents was not like this, otherwise everything would be a lot harder. Life was already hard enough.

I returned to my husband's hospital and there he was lying on his bed, it seemed that he lay in the exactly same way every time I came to visit him. It was like he never moved an inch, which made it depressing to see him. When I entered further into the room, I saw a doctor beside his bed. He greeted me with warm eyes and asked me to follow him out. Before I did, I kissed my husband's forehead. When we got outside the doctor gave me a sympathetic look and took a deep breath before introducing himself and asking if I was the wife. I introduced myself and he continued.

'Miss Collins, we are having some complications with your husband's chemo treatment. We might need to stop it.'

'Why?'

My legs began to shake. My hands were moving left and right so fast that I could not keep track.

'Chemo drugs attack fast growing cells like the ones that build up tumors. The drug travels through the body and can also attack other cells inside the body including bone marrow, hair follicles, cells in the mouth, digestive tract and reproductive system. In your husband's case the drug is not attacking the tumors but far more all the other cells. He has a genetic mutation where all cells grow quite fast. If a few cells are destroyed from the bone marrow it is not all that bad cause the long-term causes are just bone weakness, which is better than letting the tumor grow. Hair loss is another common side affect, which doesn't affect the health all too much. In the case of your husband, we don't just have hair loss and loss in bone density, but the drug is attacking all his organs and his brain. We think that if we continue he will die of chemo and not from his tumor."

I just stood there with tears falling to the floor. My knees began to feel weak. I felt them bending and there I was sitting on the hospital floor. I tried to wipe the tears from my face. Everything around me was blury.

'What are you going to do?'

'We are unsure at the moment, because cases like this don't occur frequently. That is why we are notifying you so we can discuss the options all together.'

I did not know what to do. I was afraid, more afraid than I had been previously. What was I supposed to do now? I was even considering the drug from Miss David. But that was my last resort and I felt dumb even considering it. I did not even know if I could call that a plan or if I could even consider it.

'I am so sorry to tell you this.'

I just nodded without finding the right words. I would have just loved to slap the doctor in the face, even though it was not even the tiniest bit his fault, but there was no one to blame here and that was stressing the hell out of me. I would need to find something to punch to get my aggressions out. Why did all of this need to be happening to me when there were like billions of other husbands out there that could have chemo complications. I did not want to wish harm on others but why couldn't his cancer just not say 'adios' and leave me alone. I went in to my husband in the hope he could calm me down. Make all the things go away. But how could he? He was the cause. I should not be blaming him, there was no one to blame here.

'Hello dear, how are you feeling?

'Ok.'

'Did the doctor tell you?' he asked.

I just nodded once again and went on with my crying. I could not stop myself. What was I going to do with my life? I could not bear staying in this state, I was destroying myself this way. Inside and out. There had to be some way for me to make this right, there just must be. I could not stand watching my husband fading away I had already lost enough of him. I could not lose even more. He was my everything. With and without all the lies. He was what I looked forward to come home to after a hard day of work. What would I do if he was not there anymore? I would come to the house and be alone with no one there to talk to, no one there at all. I know he would just say that I would find love again but sorry I did not want that. I only wanted him. Would I divorce him before he died so I would not need to be a widow? I did not want to be an old ugly cat lady that watched through the widow the whole day. Why was I even thinking like this? He was going to make it; I was going to dig up every cancer treatment out there. I would make him eat kale for weeks if that was suppose to help. I would go pray in the church even though I had not been in years. I would quit my job, just look after him the whole day. I was going to make this work. He was going to get better. I tried telling myself.

I got home and just stopped straight in with my dirty shoes and flopped on the sofa. And cried till there was no more water that could come out. I As was lying down on the couch and just rolled off onto the floor. My mind would not stop tormenting me. Constantly some sort of thought was bugging me in some way. I felt hopeless. I did not know what I could do. After I had left the hospital, I had called Brice's mom and we had talked for over two hours about everything. She had given me the contact number for his daughter and had told me to do what I wanted with it. But what did I want to do with it? I did not know. I thought of reaching out to her but I was just so unsure. Brice's mom thought she would have the right to know her father. I completely agreed with her but I did not know if I could handle it. I did not know if I would be messing with people's personal business again. I did not know what Brice wanted and I don't think he knew himself. I wanted to talk to someone but I felt that everyone was dealing with too much. They could not deal with me right now. I tried telling myself all I could do is concentrate on my career now. I could not influence everything that happens but somehow I was not convincing enough and I would drop back into the thoughts that broke me. But what had I done? Without thinking I googled the name of the girl to see if I could find out anything about her. I stumbled across pictures of girls in cheerleader outfits. Which one could she be? I felt some sort of connection to this girl, like I was her mother. I tried to find some similarities to Brice. I found an article from West New York middle school where she had apparently performed in a theatre group. I kept wondering what kind of person she must be. I went back and scrolled further down the site and then my eyes flicked when I saw a psychiatric unit's site. I scrolled back up this time at a slower pace and hesitated before I pressed the link. At first, I did not see anything but when I scrolled down there was a picture of a girl with red hair and green eyes. Under it I read in memorial of Alice Wilson. Was this really her? This could not be her, it must just be a coincidence. Brice would know if it was like this. It was not, she looked nothing like him. This was just another poor girl, nothing to worry about. I was worried even though I had no clue who the person was in the picture.

Well, it was a Alice, I did not know if it was the Alice, Brice's daughter. I wanted to call Brice, but I knew it was not the right thing to do right now; it would not do any good. Not at all. I would just be giving him extra stress he did not need. I wondered if this girl in this picture could be her. I could just not stop thinking. I wanted a conclusion. I wanted everything to be clear in my mind. I asked myself again if I should call Brice to ask. But I decided that it was a bad idea.

I wondered if the drug was worth taking into consideration again. What other kind of choices were there? I stared googling cancer in every language I knew, trying to figure out all the knowledge that was out there, till the point where I started coming across conspiracy theories almost. I read that just by cutting butter out of your diet you would be on a good path to fight cancer, or it was suggested to start praying on the side of the bed.

I was not religious, I believed there was something up there, but I was not going to fall on my knees and pray my heart out. Or maybe I would? What if I was in such a huge despair if Brice died that I would end up in a sect. He was not going to die, he was going to be fine. My eyes were starting to close. I had been reading sites for hours. It was four in the morning, how was I going to get up to get to work for tomorrow, well, today? How was it even possible that I had been concentrating for this amount of time? In college, I had never been able to just sit for hours and stare at my computer. I had spent this amount of time looking for something, but I had not gotten one step further. Either I had already known about it or I could eliminate it cause it was bullshit. I went on reading even though my eyes kept falling shut.

My fading attention returned in full gloom when I stumbled upon an article from Jonson&Jonson, it featured a student named Mia David who had just started working there, who had started developing a new drug to treat cancer. This was the Miss David who was in the hospital. I stared at the picture to make sure it was the same person. But I was certain. I scanned the small figure in a lab coat from bottom to top. This was the same person. How could it be someone else? So, she was telling the truth the whole time. I was intrigued and more interested then ever, I continued following the lines with my eyes, examining every word that was written in black and white. It stated that this drug was going to revolutionize cancer treatment and that only a brilliant mind could have come up with something like this. I did not know what I should do. Maybe I should just let the newly gained information sit for a day? But there was no time to be lost. By the time I had made my mind up to process it for a day I looked at the clock. I should be on my way to work. I grabbed my things and ran to the car.

I got there just in time. I could go talk to Miss David today, but when I got in the hospital, I saw that I was assigned to the back to package blood samples and send them to the lab for examination. The building where this was done was on the other side of the hospital grounds. How would I be able to sneak over? During work I did not manage to go over but I thought I could go when I finished. But it was not my lucky day. One of my coworkers wanted to go out for lunch after work and I could not talk myself out of it. I was really annoyed. After I had finished my small talk and my bagel sandwich, which was ten times better than the sounds put together to form words that I had to listen to, I went to the hospital to see my husband. I entered his room and saw him sound asleep. I did not want to wake him so I went in on my tip toes. I sat down beside his bed and placed my laptop on the night table. I was going to read more on the internet. I wanted to figure out more about this drug. Tiredness overcame me and my head kept dropping, and against my will my eyes would fall close. Reading became harder and harder, to a point where I was unsure of where and what I was reading.

'Honey."

I must have not being paying attention to him at all.

'Yes,', I answered and opened my eyes wide.

'I think you should go home, you look really tired.'

Had he been watching me without me noticing? And if so, how long?

'No way I am leaving you.'

'Its for your own good. You need to get a good night of sleep.'

'I cant sleep alone.'

'Yes you can. Just imagine I'm there lying beside you. You've got a great imagination. You can let me do whatever you want in your mind.'

'Its not the same.'

'Sure, but maybe its even better. Look you can imagine me sleeping beside you without my annoying snoring. You can make me touch you exactly where you want me to with your imagination, cause your controlling. Try it.'

'Is this what you do when I am gone?' I asked.

I was not into picturing him, it was not real, and me knowing meant it couldn't work ...

'Just try it.'

'How about I try it right here beside you?', I asked.

'You're ridiculous.'

I pretended to close my eyes and imagine the thing I so desperately wanted again. But in reality, I was lying there with squinted eyes staring at my husband who looked so terribly ill. At that moment I did not feel attracted to him. I felt the opposite. I felt disgusted, repelled by him. But why? I loved him more than anything, or was that just what I told myself? I was not sure. But for sure I had loved him when I married him. There was no doubt about that, was there? I hated myself right now. I hated everything. Nothing seemed to be going how it was supposed to. I had my whole life planned out and everything was upside down now. It was the same feeling as when I would open the dishwasher and someone had mixed up the correctly aligned plates, just worse, a lot worse. I wanted to have a family, I wanted to have continued in medical school, I wanted to have had a pet, I wanted to have not been kept from secrets, but what had

I ended up with? A husband in the hospital, a secret stepdaughter kept hidden from me for years that maybe was dead. I still worked as a nurse. I had never gone back to school and I had no children and no pets.

Soon I was going to be alone. I did not know how long he had I had to be realistic. I was going to end up sliding into depression. Why did he look so ugly lying here on the bed? He used to be soo hot. He was smoking hot. I just wanted to fall asleep honestly and even here beside him I could not. Usually it was so easy, since I felt so safe in his presence, but he was making me anxious and I could not lay still. I was constantly turning and flipping in the tiny bed while he lay there lifeless. I could probably give him a blowjob and he would not change his expression.

I did not even recognize myself, the way I was talking to myself, as if I had taken a time capsule back a few years to my youth. I should really get the fuck out of here, have a bottle of wine and watch some stupid movie or some porn. Why not? I was a mess anyway. I could let go of my perfect self. I could start again another time, I could try to be ambitious again another time. Life was bullshit anyway. I drove home, got a ticket on the way: But fuck it, it was the first ticket I had gotten in my life so honestly who cared. I didn't.

I phoned the Taiwanese around the corner on the way home and ordered everything they sold that was deep-fried. I got home and opened my bottle of wine and also poured myself some shots of vodka. And by shots, I mean glasses of vodka, I lined them up them nicely and took one by one. The deep-fried stuff was sickening but I stuffed a few more pieces in after gulping down the alcohol. I turned up the stereo system and just screamed out of my lungs. I needed this escape.I am sure I was pretty drunk when I came to the conclusion to drive to the club. Thank God I did not get into an accident, however, maybe it would have been better, then Brice and I wouldn't have needed to worry about anything again. We would have been able to meet in heaven.

I woke up to the smell of French toast; I looked around my room. it was a wild mess. I must have fallen a few times when

I came home yesterday. But what had created this untidiness? I think I had taken a few shots and then walked home. I could barley remember what had happened. I had left the house and gone to the club. But which club? What had I done? I thought and thought but nothing smart came into my mind. I checked out the window. For sure that was the case, my car was not parked outside. Thank God I had walked home and not driven, surely, I would have ran over someone. I was going to get myself together. Rest today and then get on with life. I had come to the conclusion to ask Miss David about the pills. She might be a crazy person but who cared, maybe she was a genius. The article had given her credibility. And I did not need to feel stupid about considering it. Maybe she had been different before she jumped out of the window. I could really go for a French toast. What would my neighbors think if I would just go knock on there door and ask for one. Would they think I was insane or too poor to make my own toast. Don't do it. I could just go to the cafe; that was a good idea. I would get out of the house and enjoy some food. I flung the blanket to the other side of the bed. To my surprise, I was wearing nothing at all. That was odd, I must have been extremely drunk. I put on some closes that were on the top of the piles on my shelf and went down the stairs. The smell got more intense. The scent of butter and cinnamon circled up my nose. Had I left all the windows open so that the smell seemed so close or maybe they were making French toast outside on there grill? The air also seemed to have that kind of moisture when someone cooked and did not turn the fan on. Was I dreaming? I walked into the kitchen and let out a massive scream. There was a a guy in my kitchen bare naked, wearing the apron from my grandmother, flipping a French toast. What the fuck! I turned around and ran back upstairs. I could hear steps following me.

I ran into the bathroom, locked it sat down in front of the door. My heart was racing 100 miles an hour. What had happened? I did not just have a one-night stand did I? No way! That would ruin everything. I felt so irresponsible. I felt the door push against my back. Was I stupid enough not to have closed the door properly before locking it? This guy peered around the door and looked at me. I felt like he was hunting me down, like I was his prey. I felt frozen. I could not move. The purest dread had hit me ... This was a dream. I pinched myself, hoping to wake up. What had I done. Had I lost my mind completely?

'So you want to play games again,' the mysterious man said.

Who was this guy and what was he thinking? I looked up and all I saw was his huge you-know-what dangling right in my face. I closed my eyes and wished everything away. He grabbed me. He had huge biceps. He was quite beguiling. He has very good looking. Where had I picked up a guy like this? He flung me on to the bed and pulled off my pants then slowly slipped off my underwear. I wanted to stop him, but the way his hands were moving along my legs I just did not want to anymore, it felt so good. I must have been so fucking horny. I must have been completely off my track but honestly what would have anyone else out there done? There was this knockout hot guy seducing me in one of my bad moments of life. He was making me feel so good. He was making me feel like a fucking goddess. In my grandmother's pink apron, he threw my underwear across the room. He seemed to be a professional. No wonder my room had been such a mess the morning. I whis I could remember what had happened yesterday.

He kneeled over me and lifted my sweater and started kissing me all over underneath till he reached my bra, then he changed his speed and ripped the sweater off of me. He grabbed my neck and stuck his tongue down my throat. It sounds rough in my head if I think of it, but this guy he knew what he was doing. He let his hands wander down the back of my back and stopped them right before my ass. All I was thinking was: put them on further. I did not know if he was purposely waiting there to make me want more. I slid my hands under my back and adjusted his hands right there where I wanted them. He started massaging my ass and all I wanted was more. I wanted more I wanted more of him. He slowly moved back down my legs, touching each inch of my body. His face had landed between my legs. He pushed my legs to the side and let his face descend even closer to my vagina. He definitely had found my g-spot. I think I had never had such good oral sex, such good sex not even with my husband.

So here I was with a man I did not know having the best time of my life. He suddenly stopped and ran down the stairs yelling, the French toast. I can't burn the French toast!

I did not care if that toast was burnt or was overly-soaked in egg. I did not care if the fire alarm went off. I just wanted that guy all over me again. I saw him running down the stairs, his bare buttocks bouncing up and down. He had a nice ass. He must work out. He did not come back any time soon. Maybe it also just seemed like forever to me so all I put on were my slippers and I slid down the stair railing into the kitchen. He caught me at the bottom and swung me up and sat me down on the sofa. He covered me with a blanket and kissed my ear before going in the kitchen and coming back with two plates of warm delicious smelling French toast. Who was this guy?

'Thank you,' I said.

'Anything for my princess,' he said, meanwhile giving me some more tongue.

I did not even know his name. I think we had sex another three times that day before he left, running, telling me he had to get to work. He was a bartender. I just lay on the bed naked, thinking about what had happened the last few hours. I was shocked about the fact that I had gotten so drunk and that I had had a one-night stand or a bit more than a one-night stand. I did not know if I was ok with it or not. I could not deny the fact that I really had enjoyed it. Somehow, I did not even regret it, but it was not right that was for sure. I could not even make myself feel guilty though. I just felt great, I felt like a bad bitch queen, that's the best way I could describe it. I was able to forget everything for a bit but slowly everything was returning, and I was re-entering into the dark reality. Eventually I must have fallen asleep cause the next thing that destroyed my dreams that were put together from the events that occurred that day, was my alarm. Today I was getting back to being serious in life. I got up, cleaned up a bit, got ready to go to work. Today I was going to ask Miss David about the drug. I got into the car, put on some uplifting soul classics and sang along the whole way to work. I was feeling good. I was being positive. Anything could happen, good or bad today, nothing was going to ruin my mood. It was just too good. I did not want to get down from this high. I was going to make the best out of every day from now on. I got to work humming, and Grace asked me what had happened, with astonishment.

'Nothing just happy,' I replied.

She looked at me with a suspicious smile.

'Ok then, as long as you're happy everything is good. I am proud of how well you are managing. Just tell me if you need anything, ok?'

I went on, almost skipping down the hall, greeting everybody that I saw, enjoying every moment that I had. In my break I made my way straight to Miss David's room. She was lying there, like always. She looked at me with big eyes.

'What you want now?' she asked, rudely.

Was she still mad about the mom thing? I knew that was kind of wrong but I had just wanted to do the best and nothing less. I had just wanted to help. But I was noticing that wanting to help was not always the best. Like many others also I did not always want help. Sometimes it was best just to leave someone alone.

'Look I don't care if you're still mad at me, can we just forget about it? I just want to talk about my husband's caner.'

'So I see now you're trying to get something out of me after doubting me. Look the only thing is, my drug has not been tested. It is a huge risk. Which you were not willing to take. And look, I am not stupid. I realized that you did not trust me the tiniest bit.'

'I know, I was extremely sceptical about it. I still am. I just want to talk about it. It might be my only option.'

'I understand, and I am actually willing to help you. How long do you think I still need to recover?'

'Have the other doctors not told you yet? You are being sent home in a few days. Most of the doctors tried to avoid her cause she would want them to give her an overdose of some pills or something. Of course, she had not been told yet as people tried to avoid her toxicity.

'I have not heard anything like that yet, well I don't know if I excited or not.'

'You should be.'

'For what? There is nothing out there for me. There is no point.'

'There is. It's that drug. And that can just be one out of many. There are endless possibilities in the wide world that are just waiting for you to grab them.'

'You're saying that cause you are the one who needs it. What if developing the drug won't make me happy?'

'True, but there are millions of people out there who need it, trust me. If you don't try you will never know what the outcome would be for you.'

'I know, but its just hard ok, no one understands,' she exclaimed.

'Well you aren't being clear."

'Just imagine landing in jail, working in a counterfeit factory and then failing to kill yourself and on top of that losing a friend to anorexia, as well as the man who you loved and hated at the same to suicide.'

I did not know what I should think. It was just like she had dropped a bomb over me and I had nowhere to run to. I was no psychiatrist I had no idea about this. It was a lot worse than I thought and this was without any details, just a few things.

'Everyone has bullshit in there lives.'

'I think you've told me that already. Mine is bullshit.'

'Just develop this drug then you might just find what you are looking for.'

'You are just saying this to save your husband.'

'Maybe, but not only. I am not very fond of you but somehow you have grown close to my heart.'

The more time I spent with this lady, the more sympathy I felt towards her.

'I will just take that as a positive thing.'

'It is. Look, how about ... I just had the craziest idea. When they let you go, you come stay with me. I have enough space, and I could use some company and I know you could too.'

What had just came out of my mouth with no thought at all? Was this a good plan? I had not thought before saying that. On the one hand, it was a good idea. I could manipulate her; that sounded bad. Plus I would be distracted and have some company. But on the other hand did I want her company? She was a bit odd. Well, I was taking chances lately so why not one more? If I would help her that would be enough if I got anything out of it or not.

She frowned and looked at me as if I was wearing a carnival costume or if I had just preformed a stripper move in public.

'I don't know, you don't seem to like me that much.'

'Come on.'

There was no going back now. I had said what I had said and that was how it was going to be.

'You could be some perv,' she suggested.

'I am like the same age as you are.'

'Never know."

'I am sure you've seen worse.'

I tried to convince her and I finally achieved my goal, if it was my goal. I was unsure of that. I looked down at my wristwatch and realized I had been there way over my break.

I ran out without another word. I must look like a total nutcase. Well, maybe I was at least a bit and for the moment more than I usually was, but that was fine. I was in a good mood. It was not like other days, where my dawn to dusk was filled with rain and clouds.

The day was filled with sunshine now. I finished off work and before I skipped all the way to the parking. I was starting to wonder if I had taken dugs or something last night, considering how good I was feeling. Considering I should be feeling bad cause of what I did. Or had I smoked weed, was I still high? Well, I did not know, and the new chapter of my life had begun today, so it did not really matter. It was in the past. I did not need to worry about it now. I could not change what had happened. I could only influence the future and make the best of it. If I made the best out of every day, every minute and gave my best all the time I would have nothing to regret. So, this is what I had to do and no more. It sounded like a good strategy to me. I went by Miss David's room on the way out and found her sound asleep. I contemplated waking her up but then could not bring myself to disturb her sleep, which looked so calm and peaceful. Maybe the security of being able to stay somewhere had given her some rest. When I opened my front door, a cloud of smell came out. It was difficult to identify what it was. There was a bit of French toast, some burntness, some alcoholic smell and god knows what else! I must have interpreted this scent a lot differently or the French toast had covered the odor. I entered the total bombshell; it was a complete disaster. There were clothes lying all over the house. Dishes piled high in the kitchen. Plates and cutlery scattered around the living room. A path of sheets and other items marked the route to the bedroom. What had happened was unclear, but I had fun. I, had had a party here. But the house was trashed. I got a laundry basket and started collecting the items one by one. I got the grill tongs to pick up underwear that did not belong to me. I felt repulsed picking those up. I then went on to the dishes and two hours later I had managed to make the house look presentable again.

'Are you sure about me staying with you?' Miss David asked, whose first name was Mia, I knew.

'I am certain.'

Was I or did I just want to help again? Was I that desperate? I wasn't, but I was taking a chance.

'I will pay you rent.'

'Oh please, I don't want any of your money.'

'Why?' she asked.

'Really, there's no need ...'

'Are you like, afraid of taking dirty money or something?"

'No, it's not that. Just please don't worry about it.'

I showed Mia around the apartment. It felt so awkward, like it was not even happening. It was more like a daydream. It was just unlike me. I think she was not all too surprised about the way I was living, but what was there to be surprised about? It was all pretty normal. Later that evening, I left the house alone, to go and visit Brice. I had a sick stomach, leaving Mia alone in my house. But what should I have done? Should I have taken her with me? I just kept thinking of the things she could possibly do in my house. She was a criminal, wasn't she or did that not count? I did not know. What I was thinking inviting her into my house? What kind of dullard move was that of mine? I must have been lightheaded.

DESPERATION

I felt like I was in the wrong place. I ran my finger over the dust that lightly covered the picture frames. It seemed like she had the perfect life. There were multiple pictures of her with her family or her with her husband. It seemed like she had everything the way she wanted. She had achieved so many things. I did not quite understand how I had agreed to stay with her. What had gone though my mind? I still had not found a purpose in life. Maybe I was here to save myself from killing myself again. Or least trying to. But these pictures were not doing any good to me. My mind was spinning again, thinking of all the possible things I could have done if things had been different.

I strolled around the house like a total ass freak. What the hell was I doing? I walked up to the fridge and sat down in front of it. There was a picture of her and probably her husband. It just made the tears come rolling down my face. The more I looked at it the sadder I got. I wanted to turn around and look at something else but I had to look again cause his face reminded me of someone.

I did not know who but I felt I knew someone who looked just like that. I felt it deep down in my gut, I just did not know who. I was contemplating reading the mails from my work cause I knew that I had sent them emails saying that I was in hospital. I did not want any pity. I just wanted to go back, finish that drug and die. That's all. What else did I want? Nothing. Well, actually, if I thought about it there were a lot of things but I wouldn't get them. I was just not good enough for those kinds of things so there was no point thinking about them. I was being realistic with myself nothing more or less.

I would just have to accept that I had failed in life. I had ruined myself. My personality was toxic. I intoxicated myself.

There was no question. The only person that was to blame was me, and no one else. I wished I could talk to Mike one more time. I felt like I had open drawers in my head that I could not close and that would always disturb everything else and keep things untidy. And now it was way too late to find a way to close them.

I was messed up: I missed Alice even more than I missed Mike. She had never harmed a fly and now she was less alive than the dust that travelled through the air. I longed for one more talk with her. One more hug. One more glimpse. But once again I could not have what I wanted. What was I supposed to do with myself? I was in the apartment of my nurse who I did not really know. I was all alone. I had nothing to life. I strolled over to the kitchen, picked up a knife. turned it back and forth in my hands, admiring the shining metal. The weight of it felt good in my hands, I could just stab something with full force, preferably myself. But what was the point. I put it back down and sat down on the kitchen table. The time at the hospital had not done me any good. There was no escape for my thoughts there. Just me, myself and I in a lonely room, endlessly being reminded why I was there. Then being avoided, being stamped on for being mad, then getting recognition cause they knew they would get something else out of me, something they needed. There was no other reason than the drug that I was here. Otherwise, there would have been no way she would have invited me to stay with her. If her husband didn't have a small chance with my drug, she would have been happy to get rid of me. Never needing to deal with me again. Everyone just did everything for themselves. Even donating was selfish, you did it for the adrenaline that you got from it, it was not about the starving children, not about their famished bodies. It was about the feeling the people got who sent their money overseas.

There was no such thing as selflessness; this made sense, how else would the human race be so dominant towards other species. Or, that's what we thought. I really did not know why I was here. Should I try to jump from the window again? I walked across the kitchen and turned the handle. I flung the glass out into the open air, and it nearly smashed against the opposite wall, but fell short. I grabbed the ledge and looked down to the ground. I didn't know if it was fear that caught me but I took a step back and closed the window. Was I haunted or possessed by something that was stopping me? I just could not, I could not anymore, everything was overwhelming. I continued striding through her home, but I wanted to stop myself. It was not healthy.

Ava was way too nice to me. She must have been so desperate that her husband would get better. She helped me work things out with work, which was not so hard. I wondered if my drug was so special that they did not care what I did with the rest of my life. I am sure I would have not gotten so much understanding anywhere else. If it was understanding or just weighing up the benefits and drawbacks they had or would have from me, I didn't know. In the end, it was all about the money anyhow. Not only did she help me take care of that but she made sure I was taken care off.

She set up a bed for me in the guest room. She wanted to send me to therapy, but I refused. I was not doing therapy again, that messed me up for life. If you thought about it, why would doctors want to make you healthy again if they were making money out of you? Ava had already left the house thirty minutes before to go to work. I was still sipping my coffee before I would catch the bus and to go back to work. It would be my first day since the excursion to the hospital. This would be interesting. I ran down the stairs afraid that I would miss the bus, even though I was early. I would have plenty of time. But my brain did not want to believe that, so I ran like I was running for my life. Was I? It was just a saying if I would be running for my life I would be running backwards. I made it to the bus starting to gasp for air, I didn't have much stamina. I had all the time in the world, but I kept checking the time to see that the bus was not already late. What had come over me? It was not that I was too ambitious about going back to finish my drug. But I was nervous as hell. I heard the bus from afar. It came rolling down the road and stopped right in front of me. The doors opened with a hissing sound. I stepped in, gripped a pole and rode six stops. I got off and walked in the direction of the labs. It felt like this was my first day of work. It kind of was, but I mean like the first time in my life. I did not walk through the door with the confidence I had last time, I even felt a bit embarrassed. What did they know about me? What did they think about me? I felt like all eyes were on me. I felt like I was getting holes stared though me. Was everyone watching me? I went on to the front desk, just wanting to disappear. I did not want to be here, I did not like what I was feeling.

'Good morning Mia,' a friendly voice said.

I had been looking at the floor, watching other peoples shoes. I contemplated looking up and just turning around and running out onto the busy road. But I could not do it here, not here where everyone would see. I lifted my chin so I could see the person talking to me. It was Katherine, no wonder. I tried to put on a smile but I am sure it looked fake.

'Good morning,' I replied.

'How are you feeling?"

I was so tired of this question, I did not want to answer it. No one answered it honestly anyhow. It was just something we did in society that did not make sense.

'I am fine, thank you.'

'You just need to know that we are always here for you if you need anything.'

'Thank you.'

Ya they were here for me cause they needed me, they wanted me. If I was some drug addict would they be here for me, if I was homeless would they be here for me?

'If you ever need a day off just tell me.'

'I will be fine.'

I was going to be fine, most likely. A day off would not help, that would just leave my mind more room to make up things.

'Do you want me to show you around or do you remember everything?' she asked.

'No need, thank you.'

'If you need anything tell me.'

As if I would tell her 'hey I need a life'. I need Mike, can you replay time. In my head it did not matter anymore what Mike had done or what he would have done I just wanted one last touch, and then another after that. And I wanted a few answers, even if I did not know everything, that would not be so bad. I just wanted to be with him, I wanted his company. He was the only company that I wanted. I slipped into the hole from my lab coat and buttoned up the front after I had gone through the sanitary procedures. Then I went on into the lab.

The more test I ran with my drug the more happy I got. Everything was going as planned. I realized how close I was to finishing my drug. It felt like it was not possible to have come so far. If this thing was going to work, I was a genius. The tests on cells in the lab were over and now there were just a few more things and we would test them on humans. This was the kind of study where it would take forever to find subjects. Like they had to be over 18, they had to have cancer, they needed to be willing to risk their lives. I did not know how it was going to work but I am sure they were already on the search. It would help Ava to get this drug approved as soon as possible. I could not influence that cause I did not do any paperwork. I was just the chemist. I would not be credited much for my findings I knew that, it would be the company that would get the fame and the money. Good thing was I did not want either, I just wanted one thing, Mike. Cause he would make me happy, wouldn't he? But once again I could not have what I wanted. Or if I could see Alice again, just the thought brought tears to my eyes.

'How are you holding up?' Katherine asked.

'Fine, the drug should be ready to test soon.'

'That's good to hear. I will check that everything runs smoothly. From above they told me that they want do these trials as fast and as soon as possible so by end of the week we should have our subjects.'

'Thank you.'

Katherine opened the lab door and left. In my peace and quiet I looked through my old notebook reading almost all of it. Maybe their was a note that I missed. But it did not seem like it. I had not expected that I would come to work again and everything would go so easily. I opened one of my pills and dumped the inside into test-tube where I had some isolated cancer cells. I watched them and first nothing happened but after waiting a few hours I saw lets say small bites under the microscope. They weren't perfectly round anymore. Their were small bites all around. It almost locked like Swiss cheese. It was only a matter of time till the cells would be completely destroyed. I went on too cleaning tubes, dumbing out used liquids. I think I was done. I thought about the subjects again. How were we going to find that many?

I was sure that the subjects that they were searching for would be paid a great deal of money, cause otherwise no way to find subjects nowadays. A few of course, but a whole load no way. But for money people would do a lot of things.

'Katherine do you think you could add a subject?' I asked. When I had left the lap and came past her front desk.

'I could try, why?'

'I know someone that I think would like to take part.'

'I will try my best for you. I will get back to you. But you should be on your way home now.'

'Ok.'

I was satisfied, it took me a lot to ask. I could not explain the feeling to myself. But I did it. I had asked her. Everything was starting to get real. This had been my dream. But it did not feel as good as I thought it would of feel. I entered Ava's apartment with the key she had given me. I did not know how this lady trusted me. I did not even trust myself. She was there, leaning on the wall that separated kitchen and living room. She gestured, a small wave to me as I peered around the corner of the mudroom. I took my shoes off quietly, one by one, to not disturb her call. I was doing everything in such silence that I just had to listen to their conversation. My attention peaked when I herd the name 'Alice'. Alice, if I could just go back in time and help her. I am sure I just made her condition worse. Maybe I should have never met her, maybe then she would have been better off. I even told myself then that a friend was not a good idea.

'You really need to contact them,' Ava yelled into the phone.

'Would you like it, just not knowing.'

'Honey please, I am begging you.'

'I know.'

I knew that this was not my Alice, but what if?

'I will.'

'Let me go.'

I lost interest, I could only hear her side and of that only half of what she said landed in my ear. I would need talk to Alice's family, maybe that would give me some peace. No, I would not do that. I have to stop messing people's lives up. I've just got to forget it all. I went up the stairs and lay down on my bed. I could hear screaming through my door, I knew she was getting hellishly frustrated but like what was I suppose to do? I wanted to help, but that was a bad idea.

'Mia do you want to go out for cocktails?' Ava yelled up the stairs.

We were friends now? Or was this still a benefits relationship. I should remember just not to get too close to her. I did not want to be close to anybody anymore. I could do that. I did not have much contact with people anyhow. Social life would not make me happy, I tried to tell myself.

'I don't know.'

'Oh come on, just one drink.'

She peered in and sat down beside me.

'Are you sure you want to go?'

'Yes, we can also go for ice cream or anything else, it does not matter I just need to get outside a bit.'

What was there left for me to say?'

'Ok.'

'Meet you in the car.'

And off she was. I did not know what was happening. She was acting odd towards me. Like I remember how she was in the hospital. Fake friendly like she had to be as a nurse, thinking I was crazy, like I was mad, like all I needed is therapy. It was all about therapy. I got in the car and buckled up. She pressed the gas with a bit too much force but other than that she drove smoothly. Before I could ask or comment on anything, she started gossiping away. I could not stop her; she was a stuck record.

'I don't know how your love life is but can you imagine your husband keeping stuff from you to 'protect you'? Ok, well mine thought it was a great idea not to tell me he has a daughter. Now he thinks it's a good idea not to tell her he has cancer; he thinks it will just mess things up. But that is his opinion, how about mine? He does not even want to send her a simple text or anything. It does not need to be anything big. But just letting her know would be a nice thing to do, don't you think so? What if he dies she won't even know? She has the right; she is his daughter. Now even if he does not want to what I would, she would want it. What if I want it? What if I would like to meet her, I might never have a child. I don't even know if I want children. But what if I wanted to meet her? He never asked me, did he? No that would be too complicated. My question is, what is complicated about two people meeting? However it's too late for that cause she is dead. What if she had wanted to meet her dad? What if that would have helped her? Not even I can see her. Now I will never know what kind of person she was.'

Her tears started falling, I felt bad for her but I felt like I did not know what to do. I could not even remember what she had first started talking about. I just sat there tense, not knowing how to interact. I was not the person that should be sitting there. I did not even deserve to be hearing what she was saying. Luckily, we turned into the parking lot of the bar. We went in, she had pulled herself together by that time.

IT IS A SMALL WORLD

We sat there at a table with our two cocktails and an untouched bowl of nachos. I kept wondering about this Alice. What if she actually was the same person? Before I could let my thoughts wander, she interrupted. She had been on her phone for a bit, she had been quiet as a mouse. I had enjoyed it. I did not want to tell her anything about myself. I did not want to say anything, and I was not all that interested in her life either. I did not wish to be social. I just wanted the floorboard under me to slip away.

'I keep looking at her picture,', she said.

It took me a while to realize what she was talking about.

'Just put your phone away.'

I did not really want her to put her phone away cause then I would need to talk to her. I did not feel any connection to her. I did not want to feel any connection to her.

'But look at her.'

She stretched the phone over to me. I could not believe my eyes. No way this could be real. No, no, no! My head was practically burning now. One hundred thoughts were coming to me at once. This could not be, no way. The world could not be so small. What would I do now? What was I gonna say? I could not think. I could not think straight. I could not control what was going on in my mind. I just wanted to disappear. I wanted everything to go away. Right now. I did not want to deal with it. I did not want to deal with anything at all. I could not tell her I knew this girl, but what was the point of lying?

She pulled the phone back to her chest and continued staring at the photo. I wanted to be gone. This was too much effort, too much pain. Alice had been the first person in a long time that I had actually talked to. That had lasted a bit. But like everything else it was taken away from me, just like that. I should never have met her, then I would of never of felt any of this. I wished that I had never been born to be honest, then the world would be a better place. The world did not need me, there were billions of other human beings out there. If I would not be here tomorrow hardly anyone would notice. But it felt like the world was fighting against me, there were millions of accidents a day, millions of people seriously ill. But here I was all healthy just wanting one simple thing-death, so that everything could end. I looked past Ava, who still had her eyes connected to her screen.

I checked the other people out that were sitting in the red leather booths of the bar. All of them seemed to be having a great time. There was an old couple dancing to the country music that was playing. How were they so carefree and happy? I just wish I could be there where they were. The bartender was mixing some drinks for a group of girls sitting at the bar. He grabbed a bottle of rum from the top shelf and poured in what seemed like a lot. Did he want to make those girls drunk or what? I turned back to Ava; she was still there crying. I did not know what to do, I did not want to do anything. However, I felt like it was an obligation, a responsibility to help her somehow. I placed my hand on hers.

She looked up, when I read her face I saw some kind of thank you. I don't know how to explain but that is what I saw. With her free hand she turned the phone to me again.

'Look how beautiful she is. Can u imagine, if I could have met her. I could have been some sort of support figure to her.' She burst out in tears before she could continue.

'I knew her,' I mumbled.

Why had I just said that? I could not understand myself. Once more I was doing the wrong thing at the wrong time. Could I just not shut up? The emotions started welling up and I wanted someone to shot me so I would just fall down and forget everything.

'Sorry what did you say?' she asked.

'Nothing.'

'No, tell me.'

'I knew Alice, she was in the psychiatric institution while I was there.'

'What?'

I understood that she was confused but what was I supposed to do now. I knew that I should have said nothing. I had not wanted to say anything, it had just happened, like many things. She picked up her gin and tonic and took three long sips, gulping it down.

'I met here there.'

'What was she like?' she asked.

What was she like? I asked my self. She was this sassy, crazy girl. Who had a huge heart, who had so much potential, who was strong. She was irreplaceable and she was gone. I was disposable, I was not special like her.

'She was always very curious about what people had to say. She was a very social person, she loved talking but also listening. She was a great person, her heart was huge.'

I started missing her, again. I had thought that I had been able to forget her but here I was sitting at a round table in a bar with a lady I did not know and an untouched drink. I followed her lead and chugged half the rum soda down at once. Maybe this would help.

'I wish I had met her.'

I wish I had never met anyone, what was the point? Every time I met people I destroyed them and with that myself. I was fighting myself, could I just not end that fight by defeating myself? I only saw one way of doing that, there only was one ...

'Mmm.'

'Would you come to the memorial service with me?', she asked.

I did not know if I wanted to. No, I did not want to. I did not need even more pain than I already had.

'I don't know,' I replied.

'Please.'.

'I'll think about it.'

I would think about it, but I did not want to think about it. I just did not want to go. I would have to make that clear to my brain. I did not want to play any tricks on myself. We sat there for another half an hour in silence. At least that. I could not of endured talking to her anymore, talking to anyone. Except maybe Mike. He was gone too. I just wanted to see him. When I thought of him, I felt tingling all over, but also felt hurt. I was in pain not seeing him. I did not know. It was too much. Everything was too much.

I was in my lab again. The drug was ready. Or that's at least what I thought. I did not really know what to do anymore. I cleaned everything up and just sat around for a bit. I did not feel any final relief. I did not feel accomplished. I had imagined being out of my mind when I would finish. It should have been my life's work. But it felt like nothing. It did not feel important. I went to the bathroom to waste some time. My back was super itchy, I felt like thousands of ants were crawling around. Up and down under my lab coat. I started scratching myself but it just got worse. I felt like there were burning hot stones on my back. I ripped off the coat and tried splashing my back with some cold water from the sink. I stood in front of the mirror holding my self up by leaning on the sink. What was I doing? It all must just be an illusion. I was probably making it all up. I turned around and looked at my back, it was covered with a big red spot, probably from my aggressive scratching. My thoughts flashed back to when I had been looking at my back in the same way in the psychiatric clinic. What had been put in my back that day. I stepped closer, pressing myself to the sink in order to see more closely. My back was red but nothing more. What was happening in my head and what was reality? I would never know. I heard the door handle and I scrambled into one of the toilet stalls. I put the toilet lid down and sat down. I buried my face in my hands and tried to clean up the mess in my head that I had created. I did not manage, how could I have? There was just too much going on. I looked up and stared at the red plastic door that blocked me from seeing out to the rest of the bathroom. Through the small opening at the bottom, I saw feet passing, walking to the sink. My head started pulsating and I held it in my hands. I just sat there. Not knowing where to go, what to think or what to do. At least my back had stopped itching. I stood up unlocked my door, washed my face with water and returned to my lab.

Katherine was waiting for me. 'Good you're here Miss David. We can start with the trial on Wednesday,' she said.

I should have been ecstatic about that, but I did not care. At least Ava would get what she wanted now.

'Great,' I tried to say with a smile.

'Here are all the documents that I filled out, I will give you a copy of them but don't worry you don't need to do anything. You have done an amazing job.'

'Thank you.'

'Tomorrow you don't need to come to the lab. You have a meeting with the top people at ten and then you are free.'

'Thank you.'

'I am really proud off you.'

She gave me a huge smile and I think she wanted to give me a hug but I took a step back.

'I need to go, if you need anything tell me. You can go home if you want if you don't need to do anything else.'

'Thank you,' I answered for the third time.

I had not known what else there was that I could say. I went to the changing rooms and slowly packed my stuff together. I stepped outside, walked to the bus station and waited. I had not imagined a day like this. I had gone through this moment soo many times before and it was nothing like this: in my imagination it had been filled with joy. I rode the bus home, just staring outside. Letting my eyes jump from right to left.

I let myself fall on my bed and covered myself with the light blue sheets. Could the nightmare end and let me wake up as a six-year-old kid. My brain hurt, my head hurt. My whole body was aching. I felt like I had lost all power. I could not even lift my arm anymore. I was like nothing, all the energy had drained out of me.

WELCOME TO REALITY

I had set three alarms to make sure I would get up, but I had not slept in the first place. My mind had been wandering to places it should not have. I had stared at the ceiling for hours just trying to concentrate on my breath, but I could not bear the sound of the oxygen filling my own lungs, keeping me alive. Nothing was resolved; I still did not understand the course of my life. All that I had wanted was gone. I longed for the touch, the touch of Mike. It did not matter what he had done I could forgive him. I just wanted to feel like I belonged. I wanted a taste of happiness, the taste I had gotten with Mike. He might be a felon, but he was the only person I felt so strongly about. The only person I would ever really care about. He was heaven in hell or hell in heaven. I got ready, trying to look presentable. Afterwards, I sat on the edge of my bed in silence. I was long ready to go but what was the point? It was only eight. I had ages. My eyes could not focus on anything and it just felt like my brain was swimming in my scull. I wanted to pull my eyes out and just see black, see nothing. I could not handle this. Why was this happening to me? The door opened and a pale white face looked around the inch-thick piece of wood. When Ava saw that I was awake, she opened the door further and stepped inside the room, keeping maximum distance from me. She looked terrible; she had probably not gotten much sleep either. But she should sleep, she was still fine, her life was not a disaster like mine. She still had hope; she still had happiness.

'Good morning, just wanted to check on you before I go to work. I'll be home late. I am going to Brice afterwards.'

I had never met her husband. was this whole situation not weird? To me it still seemed so unreal. Like what on earth was I doing?

'Ok.'

She went back out, closed the door behind her. I heard her leaving the house. As if I was scared of her I waited until I heard her start the car. Only then did I get on my two feet and make my way down to the kitchen. I had way too much time. I was not nervous, or stressed I just wanted it to be over with. I pottered around the kitchen thinking if I should eat something or do something else, but I ended up just looking at her pictures again, picturing myself with the life I should have had. I imagined being married to Mike, but like, the legal Mike. Not the one who would watch me with greedy eyes while I had to strip off all my clothes in prison. The one who would bring me a coffee and a muffin in the morning, that is the guy I wanted, the guy who would treat me like a lady, the one who would see me as an equal. But Mike was not my guy, I could not even make him into the person I wanted. Cause he was ff gone. Just gone like that, forever. Why was I not gone? FF it was 9.30, I could not miss this meeting. It was the only thing that had a tiny bit of sense in my life. Well, did it? Mia, stop being dumb, do what everyone else would do, get your ass to that meeting.

I ran down the stairs, got on the bus and waited for my station. I did not look like I was a smart ass scientist. I looked like a dumb ass. My hair was a mess, my nails a disaster, not even my choice of clothing suited. I had had all the time in the world but what had I done? Nothing at all. Once again. Nothing new, at least for me. I did not even know where I had to go and I only had fifteen minutes to get wherever I had to go. What the hell was I thinking? This would be embarrassing. All of my coworkers probably dreamed of a meeting with the big boss. Well, I did not know, I never talked to them. I did not interact, the only person I had plus minus talked to was Katherine. I was not even sure if that counted. I walked as fast as possible to the front entrance and pushed when the revolving door didn't turn faster. Who the ff invented these things, they weren't even useful. What was the point of them? I went in and Katherine was standing there, probably waiting for me. I began to feel the anxiety and stress that had been missing before. Maybe I only felt it cause I thought I was meant to feel it. Or was there something real inside of me?

'Good morning, follow me Miss David'

She gave me a judgmental look and checked me from my toes to the hair that stuck up in the air. Was it her problem that I showed up like this? It was not, however, she did not even look surprised. Maybe disappointed. I don't know. I did not care either. This was my time to shine wasn't it? I followed her through corridors up elevators and finally into a conference room where some men and one woman were sitting. I started to feel scared I just wanted to turn around and run away, but what was the point of doing that? I was sweating but I felt super cold at the same time. I just wanted to melt away like a candle that had been sitting in the sun for too long. No, that would take too long. More like an ice cube thrown into boiling water. I was a nobody; these people in front of me were somebodies. They had meaning in their life. They were important. Unlike me. Katherine was more important, she looked more important. I had developed the drug for cancer, but it was not mine, it belonged to the people above me. I would be mentioned in like one paper and that was it. All the credits would go to the company and its managers. It did not matter that I had done all the work. The work I was paid for. What did my salary matter if they would make millions from my pills? They would make them unaffordable for the poor, only the rich could afford them. We would have people suffering not getting the treatment they deserved, that would cure them, just cause we had CEOs and whatever's that wanted one thing, money. But what did a human life matter? Mine did not matter.

'Miss David, welcome. Have a seat.'

'Thank you,' I said.

I sat down and as soon as I had safely placed my buttocks, Katherine gave me a smile and closed the class door. The room was phenomenal. Huge windows looking over the city that was further away. If you directed your eyes lower you saw the garden, or the bits of green that surrounded the facilities. The one elderly man who was sitting in the middle faced me. He started speaking and introduced me to everyone sitting at the other end of the table. I felt intimidated; these were the people who called the shots here, the people who mattered. I was a nobody compared to them. But. I wanted to be a somebody, I wanted to be someone to myself, I wanted to be important to myself, but I wasn't. They opened a presentation and a picture of people of all ages appeared, all looking happy. Cleanly dressed, mostly in white and light clothing.

'Miss David, this is a picture that we want to use to launch your drug.'

At least they had said my drug. Cause it was mine wasn't it?

They talked about how the trials would go, and the marketing, and they asked me questions on the drug. The meeting was boring. All my initial fears had faded cause there was nothing to be afraid of. It was already all set up. These people did not care about me. They did not care what I said, how I sat there. All that mattered to them was that this drug came on the market, and they got richer. I was not surprised that men were in the majority. They had more power, privileges. It did not mean that they were smarter, better or faster. They just had been born with the right gender. Some claimed that it was God's will and that men were superior to women. But that was just an excuse. They had to give some explanation and they were just not smart enough to come up with a better one.

Finally, they gave me somethings to sign. I was hoping this meant that the meeting would be over soon. I had had more than enough of this. These people were fake. Smiling at me the whole time, pretending like they cared, pretending like I was something special, like I had qualities. Acting like I mattered, but I did not, it could be someone else sitting there and they would not care. The documents included the credits that would go to me for this drug, the money I would receive, other things, some fraud thing. I did not even really read it, cause what did it matter? If I did something I was not allowed, who cared? It would not be the first time that I would be doing something against the law. If I got one thousand more or less would it change anything for me? I had enough on my bank account, which I did not use. It was just a number. They thanked me and finally I could leave. But after the first relief of it being over I realized I still had the whole day to get through, the whole night and the whole tomorrow and the day after that and the day after that. I would still have thousands of days until the day came when I died naturally, if I ever died naturally.

I wondered how Mia was holding up. I was sitting beside my husband holding his hand as tightly as I could. I could feel the pain he was in. He was not doing well at all. He had stopped chemo; it had gone downhill. I did not know what I could still do. I loved him. I did not know how to help him. I just felt helpless here. We barley spoke, he had no energy to spare. The only thing that kept me going was that the trial of the new drug was going to start soon. I just hoped it would help. I had put all my hope into those pills. I tried to convince myself that Mia was a genius. I did not understand her, she acted so odd. But Albert Einstein was not your average citizen either. All that I could do was hope, and enjoy every minute I had with him, even though they were filled with pain. At least we had resolved our fights. I had forgiven him. Everybody made mistakes. Next weekend I would be going to Alice's memorial service. I think I would get closure on that. I wanted to say goodbye to her. I had never met her but she seemed like a great girl. I was a bit disturbed by the fact that Mia had met her, but at least I was able to get to know a few things about her. It was just a coincidence that had happened. I had been emailing with her foster parents, lovely people. I had asked them all about her, to a point where they might have been annoyed. I was sure if I just kept hoping that everything would get better. I would be back to my normal life in no time It could be better then before. I could learn from these things It was all going to be fine. I just needed to stay positive. I felt pressure on my hand, I stopped looking down to the floor with half- open eyes and turned to look at Brice. He had opened his eyes slightly. He tried to smile, but his muscles had gotten so weak, even the ones on his face. His body was destroying itself. His immune system was going crazy.

'Hi darling,', he said in a low voice. I needed some time to figure out what he had said.

I smiled back at him and hugged him. His arms did not move, they just lay there lifeless. I could not hold my tears back. I cried every time I came here. I tried not to cause I knew it did not make it any better for him. But my emotions were stronger, too strong for me to control them.

'I love you,' I said.

He tried to nod.

All I tried to think of was the good times, but that did not help. It just reminded me that time passes: That memories become unclear and things fade as time passes. I could not recreate the times we were on holiday, the time we were in Venice sipping wine. All were just blurred pictures, probably nothing close to reality. I wanted to go back. Why had I not appreciated those moments more? I should have known better. I hated the thought of the time I had wasted, the time I could have spent on things that really meant something in life.

DESTINATION DESTINY

Today was the day the trial started. I did not know how I felt about it. I was terrified but on the other hand, this was what I had been waiting for. They gave my husband the drug and I just sat in the inpatient visitors' room, waiting to see him. As if I had thought a miracle was going to happen after one pill. He still looked horrible. He just lay there like a lump of butter. I did not know what I had been thinking. I just pulled his cold body into my arms to feel his weak heartbeat. Again the tears. I would never stop questioning why something like this had to happen to me. All I was trying to do was live a happy life. Had I done someone wrong, had he?

I had quit my work. I could not cope with it anymore. I would be in tears half of the time anyway. The trial of the drug was going to be long and it would take a while to see any results. Mia, she was like a ghost, we did not talk much, she was very reserved. I did not know if it was me she was trying to avoid. I could not talk to anyone normally anymore. I was just miserable. The blood and flesh of this one person just meant too much to me. It such an important ingredient in my life. I could not do without it. I was not the same person as before. I did not feel kind anymore; I did not feel worthy anymore. I did not know how to explain. I felt like my whole life had passed before my eyes without me realizing how great it was till it got shit. There was no better word, everything sucked now. Everything. I visited him every day and never got better, always the same. I would sit in the hospital for hours, waiting for one sign of life then waiting for the next. The nurses were worried sick. I was told multiple times to go home, to take care of myself. But I couldn't. I did not want to feel selfish. I felt selfish already cause he was the one suffering and not me. And here in my very own home the girl or woman

I had tried to save, the one I had tried to help was thriving in life. She was probably living her best life; she was in the news daily. She was being interviewed, getting awards. Her drug had not even been proven to work and everyone was already hyping it. She had gotten promotions and was getting so much recognition. I did not know if I was feeling jealous or if it was nothing at all. One day she came to me while I was emptying a bottle of wine. Again. To tell me she was moving out.

'Thank you for everything, but I feel like I should move back into my apartment. You have too much going on here and I don't want to put more weight on you then you already have,' she said.

'Ok. It's up to you.'

At this point, I did not want her here anymore. I was fed up; she was just leaving me alone after all I had done for her. She was leaving me to rot away. I just wanted someone to make me feel safe again, like Brice had. I wanted to feel like I was loved, like people cared as I cared about them.

'If you ever need anything you can tell me. Thank you, you don't know how much this meant to me. I hope your husband gets well. I will make sure he gets the best of the best care.'

'Thank you.'

And there she was, gone to live her own life. I felt I was on my own, even though my family asked me every day how I was doing and tried to do their best. I felt unloved uncared for. I felt like they felt it was an obligation. It felt like they weren't doing it out of their own will.

'Hello dear, come to the hospital. I will be waiting for you at the front,' it was Brice's mom calling.

'Why?'

'I'll explain it to you when you get here,' she said over the phone.

'Please.'

Maybe he was better? Maybe he was dead, No No he was not? My mind was racing, filled at once with anxiety and hope.

I was already on my way to hop in the car. I drove faster than I should have keeping her on the phone. I got there parked my

car and parked awkwardly, jumped out and ran up to her, dropping my phone and leaving it there to be stepped over in the
grass. She stood there in tears, hugged me and took me by my
right hand and led me into the hospital. We did not say a word.
Everything seemed to be happening in slow motion. Our hands
were shaking simultaneously. It was like the silence explained
the situation we were in. She pushed open his door and I saw his
dad and some of his friends surrounded around his bed. I let go
of her hand and a path was made free for me to pass. I touched
his face, gripped his arm. Tried to shake him awake. Cried out
into the air, beginning for something to happen. There was no
response no reaction at all. His heartbeat was barely there. I
just lay beside him and hoped he would continue fighting for
me. I needed him.

'I love you,' was the only thing I had for him. Then he faded
away slowly in the next coming hours. I did not cry, I couldn't.
Just my eyes were burning, they were on fire. He could not really be gone, that was not possible. I had been frozen for hours.
There was nothing I could do about it. Some people had left, and
some had come. I had not noticed. I felt like all my insides had
been ripped out of me. I felt like I had lost everything. It was
all over now. No where was I? I did not know who I was without him. For so long I had been with him. I did not know how
to function without him. I felt someone wrap me into a hug. It
was Mia, and finally after hours of keeping the tears in I cried.
Both of us did not say a word. There seemed to be some sort of
understanding without words. It felt like she got me. I felt like
she understood without understanding, it was refreshing. No
questions I had to answer, nothing. Just simple attention, a
sort of protection.

I know it sounds the same as everyone says but it is like
that, as the months passed, I was able to accept it. I was not
over him, no, I still loved him. I had not forgotten him. I tried
to remember all the good moments. I was still sad, but I found
the ground that I could stand on without falling. I started to go
back to work, I applied to continue my studies at university. As

of Mia, the only place I ever saw her was on the screen. I longed to see her again, but I did not have the courage to reach out to her. The trial for the drug had ended and 95% of the subjects were cured or at least their condition had improved. My husband was part of the 5%. I wish I could say that everything happens for a reason, but I would never know why this had to happen. I accepted it, that was the most I could do. I was not able to do more. It was never going to be ok that it happened. But what is there to say it is life, and life sucks sometimes.

The author

Emilie Tschanz was born and raised in the small vil-
lage of Zweisimmen in the Berenese Oberland part
of the canton of Bern, Switzerland. After attending
primary school in Zweisimmen, she moved on to
high school in Gstaad, and will graduate with her
Matura in 2022. In addition to her keen interest
in writing, Emilie is a high-level competitive sailor.
She is a member of the Gstaad sailing club and in
2018 was selected for the Swiss Talent Pool of the
Swiss Sailing Team. In addition to sailing, Emilie
loves travelling, horseback riding and weightlifting.
As well as these activities, Emilie works a series
of part-time jobs – as a cashier in a gas station,
as a waitress in a restaurant and as a tutor. Emilie
Tschanz is a keen writer and Coral Eyeshadow is
her first work of published fiction.

The publisher

He who stops getting better stops being good.

This is the motto of novum publishing, and our focus is on finding new manuscripts, publishing them and offering long-term support to the authors.
Our publishing house was founded in 1997, and since then it has become THE expert for new authors and has won numerous awards.

Our editorial team will peruse each manuscript within a few weeks free of charge and without obligation.

You will find more information about novum publishing and our books on the internet:

www.novum-publishing.co.uk